CHANGING HER RULES

RULES OF LOVE

BOOK ONE

DEIDRE - ANN ANDERSON

CHANGING *her* RULES

DEIDRE – ANN ANDERSON

OTHER BOOKS BY DEIDRE – ANN ANDERSON:

CONSUMED BY HEAT TRILOGY

Sparked

Ignited

Engulfed

Falling For Heat - (Clean Version of The Trilogy as A Standalone)

NIGHT CAP NOVELLAS:

Willed to a Dom

The Dom She Needed

RULES OF LOVE SERIES

Changing Her Rules

Breaking Her Rules

"If I had a flower for every time, I thought of you... I could walk through my garden forever."
—Alfred Tennyson

CHAPTER 1

There are three cardinal rules for getting over an ass wipe of a man who treated you like shit:

1. Never stay home and mope over the sorry motherfucker that didn't deserve you. Instead find your tribe. Whether that be your girlfriends, sister, or in my case, both. Avoid shutting yourself off from the world, it will only lead to shit you'll regret or can't climb out of.
2. Find a rebound to screw with. But never anyone famous. Never anyone you work with. And never, anyone that is affiliated with or related to the ass you're trying to forget. That will only lead to further complications.
3. The most important rule of them all, never ever go catching feelings for the rebound.

. . .

MY RULES ARE TRIED and true, developed through years of picking up the shattered pieces of my heart and gluing them back together. Heartbreak is a bitch, but she's taught me a thing or two. Like how dwelling on what was, instead of focusing on what will be, only leads to misery. And trust me, I've had my fair share.

So here I am, out on the town with my girls, music thumping through my veins, the bitter taste of tequila on my tongue as we grind up against each other. Kamilla's hands are on my hips, guiding them in slow circles while Trina presses into me from behind, our bodies moving as one.

This is my happy place. Here, lost in the rhythm and the company of those who love me most. Here, I can forget about Jaden and the mess he left behind.

"Girl, you look hotter than the fires of hell," Kamilla whispers against my ear. "If I swung that way, I'd be all over your fine ass."

I laugh, the sound vibrating in my chest as I meet her gaze. "Well, it's a good thing you don't, otherwise I'd have to fight Trina off, and we both know I'd win."

My sister snorts, her hand sliding up to point an index finger in the center of my chest. "In your dreams. I'd ride you into the ground."

"Jesus, you two need to get laid," Natasha says, bumping her hip against mine. She's never been one for public displays of affection, preferring to live vicariously through our escapades. "Preferably by someone who isn't related to you."

"Jealousy isn't a good look on you," I tease, breaking free from Trina and Kamilla to pull Natasha in for a hug. She comes willingly, her lithe body fitting against mine as if we were made for each other.

And in so many ways, we were. We all were. Through heartache and betrayal, success and loss, my girls have been by my side. They're the family I chose, the ones who know me best, flaws and all, and love me regardless.

For the first time in the six months since Jaden and I broke up, I feel free. Like I can finally breathe again. There's no expectation here, no pressure to be anything but myself. Surrounded by the women who love me most in this world, I let go of everything that's been weighing me down.

The song changes into something with a slow pulse and explicit lyrics, and we head back to our table. I've done nothing but beat myself up and mope around for the last few months. Tonight, I'll start picking up the pieces, figure out what comes next in a life no longer tied to his. Tonight, I'm going to live in this moment.

I finish my drink in one long swallow, signaling to Trina who is about to head to the bartender for another round. Even with the light haze of the drinks I can see myself in her. Her usual huge puff is pressed, lying bone straight just beyond her bare shoulders down to a black off the shoulder dress that hugged her hips.

"Keep them coming!" I shout. "I'm getting shit-faced tonight!"

She grins in response, already swaying on her feet.

Leaning close, I confess, "I quit my job today. Couldn't handle being in the same office as them for another second."

Trina's expression turns sympathetic. "I'm sorry, Tals. But this is good, you know? I have no clue how you endured their smug faces for six whole months after they did you like that. Now you're free, you can do whatever you want, with whoever you want. The world is yours for the taking!"

She's right. As much as it hurts to admit, walking away from that job was the only choice I had left. Staying there, seeing Jaden day after day, it was killing me. Slowly suffocating the life from my body until there was nothing left of the woman I used to be.

But not anymore. I'm taking my life back, one step at a time.

Starting with this night, and the drinks we're going to keep pouring until the sun comes up.

Trina wipes a bead of sweat from her brow. "We've only been here an hour and I'm already buzzed." She smiles. "Which, for me, means it's time to party."

I roll my eyes. Trina hardly drinks, but when she does, she goes through them like water.

"I'm always down for tequila," Kamilla agrees, her head of curls bouncing as she sways to the beat in her seat.

"You're always down for anything that will get you drunk," Natasha corrects, nudging Kamilla and adjusting the dress straps being weighed down by her bosom.

Kamilla sticks her tongue out, eyes scanning the crowd. They widen suddenly, a predatory gleam entering their depths that has me following her gaze.

Oh hell.

Blaine mother freaking Dixon.

As in Blaine, my one and only hall pass 'Dick-son'.

Here.

Tonight, of all nights, looking like sex on legs with his brown sugar skin, muscular biceps, and low fade. I look away for all of a second before my eyes are finding their way back to the King of Temptation Aisle.

Fuck.

Double fuck.

This isn't supposed to happen. Choosing him as a rebound could lead to so many complications, but fuck if he doesn't look delicious in that pair of faded jeans and a grey Henley that clings to his muscular frame. Damn it, I have rules for a reason, ones that are meant to be followed, not broken.

Despite my rule about not sleeping with anyone famous, my gaze keeps straying to the panty snatcher at the far end of the bar. Tall, broad-shouldered, with a strong jaw and black bedroom eyes, he's looking at me like I'm the answer to all his prayers.

When I point him out to Trina, she whistles under her breath. "Hot damn, Tals. If that's not prime Nubian ass, I don't know what is."

"I know," I groan. "But he's been splashed all over Men's Health, Vybe and so many other magazine covers. Rule number two, remember? The last thing I need is to end up as the next headline in a tabloid column."

Trina waves away my concern, a scheming light in her eyes as she grins at me and the girls.

"You and your rules. Don't you know rules are made to be broken," Trina says, handing us all a shot of tequila.

We throw them back without question. The alcohol burns a trail of fire down my throat, leaving me breathless. Before I can speak, Trina is dragging us onto the dance floor.

The heavy bass thrums through my body as we move together, a tangle of limbs and laughter. Trina turns so her back presses against mine. We roll our hips in time with the music, grinding against each other.

Over Trina's shoulder, I catch Blaine watching us. His black eyes are hooded, lips parted. Heat coils in my belly at the thought of dancing for him like this, giving him a show, he'll never forget.

"He can't take his eyes off you," Trina murmurs, glancing at Blaine. "I think he likes what he sees."

A smug smile tugs at my lips. "Good."

After so long under Jaden's thumb, it feels good to be in control again. To see the effect, I have on a man, and to know I'm the one calling the shots.

Tonight, Blaine is mine, whether he knows it or not. And I plan to enjoy every second of bringing him to his knees.

My friends crowd around me, blocking Blaine from view.

"Girl, forget about Jaden, he was a controlling asshole," Kamilla says. "Live a little. Have some fun for a night."

"You deserve to be with someone who will put it down right," Natasha adds. "A man who will leave you begging for more."

Trina grins. "And what better way to get over a man than to get under another one?" Her gaze slides to Blaine. "Especially one who looks like sex on a stick."

"You're terrible," I tell her, but I'm laughing. Their enthusiasm is infectious, washing away my doubts and insecurities. They're right—I deserve to enjoy myself for once, without worrying what Jaden or anyone else might think.

"Fuck it," I say. "Let's do this."

Trina whoops, throwing an arm around my shoulders. "No, girl. Fuck him." She spins me around to face Blaine, giving me a little shove in his direction. I stumble, but recover quickly, smoothing my dress and stepping up to him with a sway in my hips.

Blaine watches me approach, a muscle twitching in his jaw. He looks away, but soon after his eyes are scanning my body, taking in every detail as if he wants to remember it all. His gaze lingers on my lips as I lick them and seem to sharpen with hunger.

"Hi," I purr, stopping just shy of touching him. I tilt my head back to meet his gaze, acutely aware of our height difference. Of how he looms over me, radiating heat and sex. "Having a good night?"

"Better now." Blaine's voice is a low rumble, sending a delicious shiver down my spine. "I couldn't help noticing you on the dance floor."

"I had a feeling I caught your attention." I trail a finger down his chest, relishing the way his breath hitches. "The question is, what are you going to do about it?"

His hand closes over my wrist, holding me in place. "I have a few ideas."

He rakes his dark gaze over my body. "I can't shake the feeling we've met before though."

A spark of excitement ignites in me at the promise in his

words. Tonight, I'm going to do whatever I want. Take whatever I want.

And right now, I want Blaine.

"I don't think so," I say, maintaining my flirty tone. "I'm sure I'd have remembered a handsome face like yours."

"That's it." He nods, thinking to himself. "I ran into you at my twin brother's BBQ that one time. You were there with Blair's friend. Did that ever pan out?" he asks, jolting me from my revery. "Jaden, I think his name was. Blair's bosom buddy."

A bitter taste travels up my throat, but I maintain my composure. Blair is Blaine's twin brother, identical in most features save for a prominent scar beneath Blaine's right eye, a scar that I once read was given to him by his stepdad as a child. He is constantly around Jaden, so I had no doubt he knew what Jaden had been up to behind my back. But I never stopped to think about how many of his friends had been privy to that information.

"Whatever deal I had assumed I had with Jaden ended abruptly when I walked in on him taking a deep dive into my ex-assistant's cunt," I say, a bit brasher than intended.

This was why I had rules.

Blaine's expression softens, "I feel like such an ass. I wouldn't have brought it up had I known.

My gaze falls to the floor, and he sighs.

"I've been out of town for the past few months working on a catalog spread with Men's Health. I just got in this morning," he admits. "I promise you I had no clue. If I'd known that jackass would've lost some teeth by now for disrespecting a queen like you."

That admission makes me smile. Taking the opening, Blaine leans down, his lips brushing my ear. "How about we get out of here?"

I nod, anticipation thrumming through me. We make our way to the exit, Blaine's hand warm on the small of my back. Outside, he hails a cab and gives the driver his address.

The second the door closes behind us in Blaine's house, he presses me against the wall and claims my mouth in a searing kiss. I moan, sinking into him, my hands roaming over the hard muscles of his back and chest.

He hitches my leg around his hip, grinding against me in a way that makes me ache for him. I fumble with the buttons of his shirt, shoving the material off his shoulders as he lifts me, guiding my legs around his waist.

I expect him to take me to the bedroom, but Blaine has other ideas. He carries me over to the couch, laying me back against the cushions. His hands slide under my dress, fingers hooking into my panties. I lift my hips, helping him drag them down my legs.

Blaine settles between my thighs, trailing kisses up the inside of my leg. I fist my hands in his hair, silently begging for more. For everything.

He glances up at me, eyes smoldering like burning coal. "Tell me what you want."

"I want your mouth on me," I breathe. "I want you to make me cum."

A wicked grin curves his lips. "As you wish."

Blaine dips his head, and I cry out at the first sweep of his tongue. Heat explodes through me as he lavishes my clit with attention, building the pressure inside me.

"Tell me how you like it, kitten."

I know Blaine is speaking but my brain is too scrambled to form a response.

He sucks my clit into his mouth, and I scream in pleasure. Fuck it'd been too long since I had a man claim my pussy like this. I arch beneath him, volts coursing through me in waves as he continues his onslaught. Blaine takes his time, eyes trained on me to ensure he's giving me what I want. How I like to be pleased clearly matters to him—unlike Jaden. Sex with Jaden had always been about him. And after he got his release he'd be knocked out, blissfully unaware of my pleasure or lack thereof. No foreplay, no oral, just lube, in and done. But not Blaine—he takes the time to ensure I'm enjoying every minute.

Blaine swipes his tongue over my clit once more before sliding two fingers in my now wet hole. Everything swimming in my head drowns as pressure begins to build deep inside me.

"Do you like that, kitten?"

I meet his eyes as his fingers cup to reach my G-spot. He dips his tongue back onto my clit. My head flies back and a scream lodges in my throat.

"Me-fucking-ow," I scream. "Right there. Just like that."

Blaine must've been an A-student because he runs with my instructions like Usain Bolt on the fucking 100m track. He thrusts into me faster and faster. Each time brushing the delicate flesh as his tongue circles my clit.

"Oh fuck. Fuck. Don't you fucking stop," I scream.

Blaine pulls his hand from my pussy but before I could protest his hand finds my clit, pressing and rubbing it from side to side.

"Holy fuck. I'm gonna … I'm gonna —"

I shatter with a hoarse shout of his name, cum squirting out of me in waves I never even knew was possible.

My chest heaves as I come down from the high, muscles still trembling, a girlish smile on my lips.

"You're fucking amazing. Did you know that kitten."

"Meow," I purr teasingly. "I've never been called kitten in bed before, but I have to admit its growing on me."

Blaine sits up and claims my mouth in his, my juices a mix of sweet and salty on his tongue. He leans back, breaking the kiss and returns to kiss my clit, making me shiver. The sight of him between my legs, disheveled and aroused, makes me ache for another release.

Tonight, I'm going to ride Blaine until we're both exhausted.

And when the sun rises, I'll leave with memories that will sustain me for a long time to come.

Blaine stands and strips out of his shirt, giving me an unobstructed view of his chiseled abs and broad shoulders. I lick my lips in anticipation as he undoes his belt and jeans, pushing them down his lean hips.

He's gloriously naked, cock jutting forward, thick and hard. I sit up on the edge of the couch, running my hands over his chest and down his abs.

"Condom?" I ask, not willing to risk it with a near stranger.

Blaine nods and disappears into the bedroom, returning a moment later with a foil packet in hand. I take it from him and rip it open, rolling the condom down his length.

With a growl, Blaine lifts me, hands grasping my ass as my legs wrap around his waist. He thrusts into me in one smooth stroke, filling me to the hilt. I cry out, nails digging into his shoulders.

"Fuck, you feel good," he grunts, withdrawing slowly only to slam back in. He sets up a punishing rhythm, bouncing me on his cock as I cling to him.

Blaine pounds into my pussy, his hips slapping against me with unrelenting vigor. I shudder, clenching around him.

The sheer pleasure of it all was too much for words. My primal screams fill the air, my body desperate for release. As if sensing my need, Blaine increases his speed, thrusting faster and faster.

I dig my nails into his back and slam my eyes shut as I near the edge. Unearthly colors explode behind my eyes as my climax rip through me. My opening convulsing around Blaine's cock.

He groans, hammering into me as he buries his face in my neck with a hoarse shout.

We stay locked together, panting, as aftershocks ripple through my body.

Eventually, Blaine carries me into the bedroom and collapses onto the bed with me sprawled across his chest. I know I should leave, but for now I'll bask in the warmth of his embrace. There will be time enough for regret in the morning.

CHAPTER 2

I wake with a start, my eyes blinking open to the bright sunlight streaming through the skylights overhead.

The spot beside me is cold. Empty.

Latalia is gone.

Panic rises in my chest as I sit up, scanning the room. The rumpled sheets are the only evidence of what happened here last night.

I rake a hand through my hair, trying to calm my racing pulse. She probably just went to the bathroom or downstairs to make some coffee. Any minute now, she'll walk back through that door with one of her radiant smiles and—

The house is silent.

"Latalia?" I call out, throwing back the covers. No response.

Shit.

I pad out of the bedroom on bare feet. The upper floor is empty, sunlight pooling across the hardwood. I check the guest rooms, the home office, even the balcony, but there's no sign of her.

By the time I get downstairs, panic has morphed into anger. Into hurt.

She left. Just like all the others.

The sting of rejection cuts deep. I've faced rejection at nearly every turn in my life, starting with my own mother, who cared more about her next fix than her own son. Until she couldn't cure her 'needs' with the douche bags from her whorehouse. Then she'd be all chummy again as she forced Blair or me to fill the spot.

A shudder runs down my spine with the memory and I squeeze my hands into fists willing myself to forget. I vowed not to let anyone in again to protect myself. But after the shit show of a day I had yesterday, I'd needed alcohol. And like all the other times I drank, my defenses would lower, and the throngs of women transform to seedlings of my deepest hope, the possibility of more. One look into Latalia's eyes and all my resolve crumbled.

I stride into the kitchen and spot a note stuck to the marble island. In her pretty cursive, it reads:

THANK YOU FOR A LOVELY EVENING. I had a wonderful time. Latalia.

NO NUMBER. No last name. No suggestion of seeing each other again. Just a polite brush-off.

I crush the note in my fist, fury burning hot in my veins. I'm so fucking tired of being seen as the hot piece of ass women want to jump. I should've known better than to think she'd be different. Everyone wants the same damn thing—a night with the "hot model." They don't give a shit about me. About *who* I really am.

With a roar, I sweep my arm across the counter, sending the fruit bowl and other knickknacks crashing to the floor.

How could I have been so blind?

I drag myself into the bathroom, hoping against all rationale she'll be there. But the room is empty, devoid of any trace of her. The scent of her perfume still lingers though, a cruel reminder of the night we shared.

I turn the shower on full blast, desperate to wash the lingering traces of her from my body. But no amount of scrubbing can erase the memory of her touch, the taste of her kiss, her dripping pussy, or the sound of her soft moans in my ear.

By the time I step out of the shower, my skin is raw and stinging. But I still feel unclean. Still tainted. Once more used and tossed to the side, and I'm catapulted right back to ten-year-old Blaine again. Just like I am every fucking time.

Fuck!

I slam my fist against the marble next to the ceramic basin hoping to feel anything other than emptiness. Cursing, I head to my closet desperate to clear my head.

I throw on a pair of sweatpants and a t-shirt, not bothering with anything else. My agent and PR team will have my head for missing another meeting and photo shoot, but I can't bring myself to care.

Right now, all I want is to be left alone. To nurse my wounded pride and shattered heart in peace. To pick up the pieces of myself Latalia left behind and try to cobble them back together into some semblance of a man.

But even alone, I can't escape the truth: I'm broken. And for the first time in my life, even the thought of hitting the gym in my basement offers no solace or distraction from the pain. Latalia had caught my attention from the first time I'd seen her at Blair's BBQ. She'd been so beautiful, and vibrant with a personality that lit up the entire room. Her energy was so contagious that day that it had shifted my mood despite the shitty day I'd been having without me even talking to her directly. I knew then that she was special. But at the time, she'd been hanging off that prick's arm, so I'd let her be. Telling myself that if we were meant to get to know each other we'd meet again when the time was right.

When I ran into her again last night, I was dumbfounded. I remembered her instantly but decided to play it cool. And it worked. She came home with me. Offered herself up to me like she had in my fantasies. I thought she'd felt the same spark I had. But clearly, I was fucking wrong.

I pace the length of my living room, anger and hurt warring inside me. How could I have been so stupid? So blind?

Latalia used me, and I fell for it hook, line and sinker. Let her into my bed, into my fucking head, without a second thought. Without considering the consequences.

God, the consequences. I scrub my hand over my face, trying to rub away the sting of betrayal. I knew better than to trust a woman so easily. Knew they only wanted one thing from me. But Latalia seemed different. Her interest in me seemed genuine in a way I'd never experienced before.

Fool. I'm so fucking stupid.

With a growl of frustration, I slam my fist into the wall. The sharp pain that lances through my knuckles does nothing to ease the anger brewing in my gut. The one that's been there since I realized Latalia disappeared like the mirage, she turned out to be.

I'm so tired of this. Of building up hope for women who only want my body. Who takes what they need from me, then leaves without a backwards glance.

I want more.

Deserve more.

But maybe a man like me isn't meant to find real love.

Maybe I'm destined to live my life as I do my job—a piece of meat for women to ogle and consume as they please, my heart and feelings irrelevant. The thought leaves a bitter taste in my mouth as I stare out the window at the city stretched before me.

If that's my fate, maybe it's time to get out of this game altogether. Find a new path, a new purpose. One that doesn't leave me hollowed out and hurting. One that might, possibly, lead me to a woman who wants my heart as much as my body.

A woman like Latalia.

But not Latalia.

Never again Latalia.

I shake my head and push away from the window. No use dwelling on pipe dreams or lamenting what can't be changed. For now, I need to focus on what I can control.

Namely, working out this anger and frustration churning inside me before I do something I regret.

I head down to my gym. The familiar scent of metal and sweat greet me as I walk through the door. My muscles hum in anticipation, eager to be pushed to their limits.

As I start in on the heavy bag, I fall into a rhythm.

Jab, cross, hook.

Jab, jab, cross.

Again.

Jab, jab, cross, right kick.

Again

Each punch is harder than the last until my knuckles scream and the bag rattles on its chains.

With a yell, I launch into a spinning kick. The bag careens away, then swings back to meet my fist in an explosion of power and pain.

Breath rasps in and out of my lungs as I dance around the bag, unleashing every ounce of rage inside me. Rage at Latalia. At my mother. At the world that seems determined to remind me how alone I really am.

I fight until my legs tremble and darkness creeps into the edges of my vision. Only then do I collapse to the mat, chest heaving, and body drenched in sweat. The anger and ache have dulled to a faint whisper, leaving me drained but clear-headed.

Tomorrow I'll decide what comes next in my life and career. But for now, I simply breathe through the solitude and silence. The familiar companions that never seem to desert me for long.

My phone rings, the sound echoing through the gym. I peel myself off the mat and cross over to where I left the device on a weight bench.

My agent's name flashes across the screen. I swipe to answer, bracing myself for whatever new demand is about to be placed on my time. "Trixton. What's up?"

"Blaine, glad I caught you. I've set up a meeting for you this afternoon with a new PR rep. Think it'll be a great match."

I frown, grabbing a towel to wipe the sweat from my face. "New PR rep? What happened to Sandra?" The woman had been managing my public profile for years. While not the most competent, at least she understood my preferences.

"Let's just say Sandra is no longer with the company," Trixton says cryptically. "This new rep comes highly recommended and has some fresh perspectives that will benefit your image. Meeting's at four at that new steakhouse you like."

I clench my jaw, irritation simmering in my gut. So, Sandra has been fired without anyone bothering to inform me. And now Trixton expects me to just show up for a meeting with some stranger tasked with managing my life.

"Did you at least get a name for this new rep?" I demand, keeping my tone hard. Trixton knows better than to push me on issues like this.

"Does it matter?" he asks casually. "You'll meet her this afternoon either way. I'm sure you'll both get along famously. Now, don't be late!"

The line goes dead before I can argue further. I stare at the phone, half tempted to call my agent back and tell him exactly where he can shove this meeting.

But in the end, I know I'll go. I always go where I'm told, dancing on strings controlled by people who see me as nothing more than a product to be packaged and sold.

Maybe it's time I cut a few of those strings. But for now, I'll play the role that's been given to me. Even if it's not the one I would have chosen.

I finish my workout and shower, dressing in a pair of fitted slacks and a casual button-down shirt. No need to impress my new handler, whoever they may be. Let them see me for who I really am, not the glossy illusion splashed across billboards and magazine covers.

When I arrive at the steakhouse, Trixton is already seated at our usual table, a glass of wine in hand. He stands as I approach, smiling broadly. "Blaine, so glad you could make it. Our new PR rep will be here any minute."

"You mean you still don't have a name for me?" I ask as I take the seat across from him.

Trixton waves a hand dismissively. "Minor details. I'm sure you'll get along swimmingly, regardless of a name."

I frown, watching the entrance for any sign of my mysterious new rep. A few couples filter in, followed by a group of businessmen in expensive suits, but no one seems to be searching the room for us.

Just as I'm about to suggest we leave; the door opens again. A woman strides through, her heels clicking against the polished wood floor. She scans the room, and for a moment, her familiar brown gaze meets mine, warm and knowing.

IT CAN'T BE.

I stare at the woman making her way toward our table.

My mind must be playing tricks on me.

But when she stops beside our table, smile lighting her beautiful face, I know there's no denying the truth. My new PR rep is none other than Latalia, the woman who left me behind in bed just this morning. And by the looks of things, I've been played.

CHAPTER 3

LATALIA

I take a deep breath and smooth my dress over my hips before stepping into the dimly lit steakhouse. The aroma of grilled meat and spices fills my senses, but it does little to calm my nerves.

I snuck out of Blaine's house before sunrise, careful not to wake him from his slumber. Our night together had been exciting and unexpected, and the sex ... God! The sex had been incredible. But I knew that this kind of dangerous fun would eventually lead to heartache and disappointment. Of course, at that time, I'd been of the belief I'd never have to see him again.

Blaine Dixon is more than a bad boy—he's a walking disaster based on most magazines I had read. And though that was exactly what I'd needed last night, his playboy reputation needs to be kept away from my kitten at all times. My cheeks heat at the thought of the nickname he used repeatedly while driving me up the edge of ecstasy and I shake my head in a frail attempt to clear my head.

That stays in the past. Especially since I went home to the offer of a lifetime. I needed to focus and figure out my next move. Sandra, Kamilla's cousin, had gotten herself in hot water with her client and for whatever reason needed to step away. So, she offered me the contract. And considering I'm now jobless in Manhattan, I accepted. The only hiccup was that the client in question was Blaine Dixon. The same Blaine freaking Dixon that had just screwed my brains out.

But again, I need this opportunity.

I assured her he'd be taken care of. Plus, she'd sounded so desperate as she flat out begged me to take over her largest client. Which, of course, is a no brainer. I needed to prove to myself that I could make a name for myself in this business without the influence of Jaden or his father.

Which means that while I'd prefer never to see Blaine again, nor to be constantly reminded of the multiple orgasms, or the squirting – which I didn't even know I was capable of – every second while I'm at work, it was five figures a month and mama didn't raise no fool.

My gaze scans the room and lands on a table in the far corner where Blaine and Trixton, whom I had only spoken to once via a video call a few hours earlier, are already seated, drinks in hand. Blaine's piercing eyes meet mine from across the room, and a spark of heat ignites in my core.

Damn.

I paste on a polite smile and make my way over, hoping the dim lighting masks the awkward expression that must be evident on my face. "Sorry I'm late."

Trixton stands and envelops me in a friendly hug. "Ms. Brown, so glad you could join us." His enthusiasm helps settle my nerves. At least one of them is happy to see me.

Blaine simply nods in my direction, his full lips pressed into a grim line. The memory of those lips on my skin last night flickers through my mind, and I have to clench my hands at my sides to maintain my composure.

"Please, call me Latalia," I say with a smile.

"Of course, Latalia. Please, have a seat," Trixton says, gesturing to the empty chair.

I sit, arranging my napkin in my lap. "Thank you for including me in this meeting. I'm looking forward to discussing how I can help boost Mr. Dixon's image."

A snort escapes Blaine. "I don't need your help." The bite in his tone makes it clear he is no longer under the influence of whatever alcohol he'd consumed last night. "This whole PR stunt is Trixton's idea, not mine."

Trixton shoots him a warning look. "Blaine, that's enough. Ms. Brown … Latalia is here as a professional, and she deserves your respect."

A tense silence follows. I refuse to back down from Blaine's glare, instead meeting it with a cool, level stare of my own. He may regret our night together, but he won't intimidate me. I've worked too hard to rebuild my confidence after Jaden to let another arrogant man tear me down again.

Blaine is the first to look away, grabbing his glass and draining it in one swallow. The motion draws my gaze to his throat, where a faint mark peeks out from his collar—a souvenir from my eager mouth. Heat pools low in my belly at the sight.

This is going to be a long meeting.

I clear my throat and look at Trixton. "As I was saying, I'm eager to discuss how we can improve Mr. Dixon's public image. What specific concerns do you have?"

"Blaine's reputation has taken a hit recently due to some...indiscretions on set." Trixton's mouth flattens into a grim line. "There was an incident yesterday that's caused a major PR crisis."

My gaze snaps to Blaine. "What happened?"

He scowls at his empty glass. "Nothing that concerns you."

"It does concern me if I'm trying to fix your image." I lean forward, bracing my elbows on the table. "Start talking, Mr. Dixon. Now."

His eyes flick up to meet mine, simmering with anger, but after a moment he caves. "I may have punched the photographer of my latest project in the face."

I suck in a sharp breath as Trixton groans. "Why on earth would you do that?"

"Because the pompous jackass grabbed one of the models and tried to force himself on her!" Blaine snarls. "She was terrified and screaming for help. What was I supposed to do, just stand there and watch?"

His vehemence gives me pause. While violence is never the answer, I can understand why he'd react strongly to protect a woman in danger.

"Did you report his behavior to the authorities?" I ask gently. "Press charges for assault?"

Blaine's mouth twists. "No. I was too angry in the moment to think clearly. After I hit him, I just stormed off set. By the time I calmed down, it seemed pointless. No one would believe me over him." He shakes his head and shrugs. "Not that it matters now. I'm sure I've been fired from the project and blacklisted from working in this town again."

A wave of sympathy washes over me. He may be arrogant and short-tempered, but he didn't deserve this. I reach out to squeeze his hand.

"It's going to be okay," I say, willing him to believe it. "Trixton and I will figure something out. This kind of behavior can't continue unchecked."

Blaine searches my face, a myriad of emotions flickering through his eyes. But he doesn't pull away from my touch. "You'd really help me?"

"Of course." I give his hand a gentle squeeze. "No one deserves to have their career ruined for doing the right thing."

A smile tugs at the corners of his mouth, softening his

features. "Then it looks like you're not as heartless as I thought, Latalia Brown."

My own lips curve to mirror his. "And you're not as impossible as I first believed, Mr. Dixon."

I shake my head, avoiding Blaine's gaze. The memory of his hand in mine and the warmth in his smile lingers. I clear my throat and fold my hands in my lap.

Trixton excuses himself to go to the Men's room. I shift in my seat, suddenly nervous to be alone with Blaine. Last night still lingers in my mind, and the memory of his touch haunts me. I have to stay professional, but the simmering tension between us makes that difficult.

Blaine leans forward, his gaze intense. "You think you can fix my reputation that easily? Lil Miss Save a Hitta. I'm not some project for you to 'handle.' What's your angle here anyway?" he demands. "Did you really think I wouldn't remember last night?"

My cheeks burn. I should have known he wouldn't just let it go and let us move on.

"I'm not playing any games," I say evenly. "I came here as a professional, to discuss a business opportunity. What happened between us last night was a mistake. It won't happen again."

"A mistake?" Blaine scoffs. "Is that what I am to you? Another regret to add to your collection?"

I roll my eyes before meeting his gaze. "What's your problem? You're a freaking underwear model, for God's sake, and I'm a plus-sized marketing rep. We have nothing in common. There is literally no world where we both fit together long term. I did us both a favor by leaving before things got more complicated."

"More complicated?" Blaine shakes his head. "You don't get to make that decision for me. I'm not some boy toy you can play with and discard when you're done."

"I never said you were," I snap. "But I was not going to stick around so you could kick me out this morning once you realized who you'd brought home. Been there, done that, learned from it."

"How would you know what I would've done?" Blaine demands. "You didn't even give me a chance!"

"And why should I have? So, you can add me to 'your' long list of regrets in the morning?" I challenge, turning his own words back onto him.

Blaine glowers at me. "You've got some nerve, judging me when you're so determined to push everyone away."

"I'm not pushing you away," I say through gritted teeth. "I'm protecting myself. Plus, I can't push away something I never really had. We spoke to each other for all of 3 minutes last night before we slept together."

"Protecting yourself?" Blaine scoffs. "From what? Getting close to someone who might actually care about you?"

I suck in a sharp breath, stunned into silence, his statement too close to reality.

"Don't pretend like you know anything about me."

The tension in the room is thick enough to cut with a knife. Blaine's eyes bore into me, dark and unreadable, his full lips pressed into a firm line.

I straighten my spine and lift my chin, refusing to cower under that piercing gaze. "I'm not leaving, Blaine. You need me for this campaign whether you want to admit it or not."

His jaw ticks, a muscle feathering in his cheek. "Is that right?"

"Yes, that's right. I've worked too damn hard to get to this point, and some pretty boy model isn't going to scare me off." I lean forward, close enough to see the gold flecks in his eyes. "So, grow the fuck up or grow a backbone. Either way, I'm here to stay."

The tension simmers between us, potent and electric, when Trixton rushes back over to us, flushed and breathless. "I hope everything is going well between you two. I know that will be an amazing partnership."

Trixton's enthusiasm breaks the spell. I lean back, and Blaine rakes a hand through his thick hair as he looks away. A smirk tugs at my lips, part triumph and part challenge.

"It's decided," I say, facing Trixton with a plastered smile. Blaine glances over at me and I hold his gaze. "I'd be elated to take Mr. Dixon on as a client. We'll get his reputation cleaned up in no time."

Blaine lowers his eyes and I smirk.

The air still crackles with unresolved tension, a promise of things still left unsaid. But for now, I've made my point. Latalia Brown doesn't back down from a fight with controlling men, not anymore.

And Blaine Dixon's gonna learn that the hard way.

"Perfect," Trixton says, with an air of enthusiasm I can't discern as fake or genuine. "So, I'll give you the night to prep and arrange for the movers to grab anything you need to go over tomorrow."

"Wait," I say as my brows crease. "Why would I need to move my stuff?"

Trixton's face curves to mirror my expression. "Sandra did explain the position to you, right?"

A bead of sweat runs down my forehead, and I become acutely aware of the strain of the hairpins holding my kinky curls into the sleek bun on top of my head as I nod.

"She explained that she needed someone qualified to represent Bla... Mr. Dixon," I begin, recounting all that Sandra went over with me out loud."

Did I miss something?

"She said she had to walk away from Mr. Dixon for personal reasons," I continue. "She heard I was relaunching my own firm that had been on hiatus plus we had previously worked on joint campaigns, so she knew he'd be in good hands if she recommended me. That part, I understand. But that still doesn't clarify why I would need movers." I glance over to Blaine. "Is there an international shoot she forgot to mention?"

Trixton visibly hesitates then sighs.

"That is all accurate," he begins with a pause for too long for comfort. "But that's not the entire job description."

Blaine's brow rises slightly which tells me he's just as baffled as I am at this point. At least there's still a level playing field, but what did I just commit to?

"I don't follow," I admit.

"Due to the extreme circumstances surrounding Blaine's current public image," Trixton begins again, "the agency has decided to employ a bit more of a hands-on approach to repairing his brand." Trixton pauses to glance over to Blaine then takes a gulp of the water that had been sitting in front of him untouched for the entire meeting. "The role we're seeking to fill is for a 'live-in' PR representative. You'd be moving to a guest room in Blaine's home."

My jaw drops.

"Like fuck you are," Blaine exclaims, spinning to face Trixton so fast he all but knocks over the table. "I do not need a fucking babysitter."

Trixton glances around the restaurant. All eyes and phone cameras are on us and the spectacle that is Blaine Dixon.

"I'm pretty sure the headlines over the next 24 hours would disagree," Trixton counters, so calmly a chill ran through me. Besides, right now you do not have a choice. The agency has already met. There are two options on the table. Either you agree to have a living PR Rep. Or I can't represent you anymore. It's your choice."

Blaine's Adams apple bobs but he says nothing. He avoids meeting my eyes. There's something in his expression that tells me he needs to keep his career more than he's letting on. But of course, he's too stubborn to admit that he's wrong.

Blane meets my eyes, but he says nothing.

"I'll do it," I blurt out before I could talk myself out of it.

Trixton beams. "Brilliant, then it's settled."

This is madness, I know. But I have to take charge of my life and I want to make a name for myself in the industry I'll need a high-profile client. He's just a client. A client I already fucked and will now be seeing on a daily basis, but still just a client.

I can do this. Right?

CHAPTER 4

LATALIA

I trudge up the creaky stairs of our walk-up, the familiar ache in my knees from the day's heels and meetings throbbing with each step.

Our apartment is small but cozy, mismatched furniture scattered about the living room Trina and I have shared for five years. The lingering aroma of her latest baking experiment—something with chocolate and raspberries—wafts over me as I step through the door.

"Tals!" Trina spins on her heel, her curls bouncing around her heart-shaped face. She rushes over and envelops me in a hug, the warmth and familiarity of her embrace soothing my frayed nerves. "How did it go? Did you blow them away like I knew you would?"

I sigh and lean into her, the events of the day crashing over me. The meeting had gone well, better than expected, but the confrontation with Blaine afterward still leaves a bitter taste in my mouth.

You're being ridiculous. It was just sex—mind-blowing, toe-curling sex, but sex all the same. I have a strict no-repeats policy when breaking my rules for a reason.

"The meeting was a success," I say, keeping my tone light. "But Blaine wasn't too happy with me for slipping out before he woke up."

Trina pulls back, eyes narrowing. "What? You don't owe him anything. What an arrogant jerk!"

"I know, I know. It's fine. The account is mine, if I want it, that's all that matters." I make my way over to the sofa with a groan and sink into the cushions.

Trina sits beside me, the springs creaking under her slight weight. She takes my hand, her fingers warm and strong. "Did he do something to upset you? Because if he did, I swear—"

"Nothing happened." My stomach twists at the lie. I can still feel Blaine's hands on my body, his lips branding my skin. I swallow hard, chasing the memories away. "He was just annoyed I didn't stick around for breakfast. But it's done now."

If only it were that simple.

Trina squeezes my hand, her eyes soft with concern. "Are you sure you're okay? I'm here if you want to talk about it."

I smile, a rush of affection for her sweeping over me. She knows me too well, can see right through my flimsy façade. But this is my battle to fight. I've already broken one rule—I won't break another by unloading my troubles onto her.

"I'm fine. Just tired." I stand, release my bun with one hand while ruffling her curls with the other. We both laugh as she swats at my hand.

"I'm going to change for bed." I say. "Don't stay up too late."

"Yes, Mom." Trina sticks her tongue out at me before turning back to the TV.

I slip into my room and close the door, sagging against the wood. Blaine's face floats behind my eyes, all rugged jaw, delicious brown sugar skin and piercing eyes, and I grit my teeth against the surge of heat the memory elicits.

One night. It was just one night. I got what I wanted—the account and mind-blowing sex.

Now it's time to move on. Sighing, I push all the memories of Blaine and the guilt of not telling Trina I'd be moving out tomorrow to the back of my mind and force myself to sleep. Tomorrow will be a new day. I just need to get a good night's rest to tackle everything tomorrow.

"Tomorrow," I repeat to myself before closing my eyes and allowing sleep to wash over me.

I wake with a start, heart pounding. For a moment, I'm in bliss as the familiarity of my bedroom engulfs me.

Then it hits me. After today this won't be my home anymore. I'll be waking up in Blaine's massive and hollow house. The memories of last night rush back in a flood.

The meeting. The tantrum. The realization I'd have to move in to handle his account properly. Trina's concern, my half-hearted reassurances.

What a cluster fuck.

I sigh as an image of Blaine fills my mind, all hard muscle and hungry eyes. I slam my eyes shut to drown my thoughts.

Forget Blaine like that. One night, I reminded myself. No exceptions.

I can handle this—I handled Jaden, didn't I? I just need to remember the rules. Blaine is a client, nothing more. Keep things professional, push any non-business contact to the side. Even if it kills me.

With a groan, I throw back the covers and get to my feet. Time to face the music.

I find Trina in the kitchen, singing along to the radio as she makes coffee. She turns when I enter, a smile breaking across her face, but it falters at my expression.

"What's wrong?" she asks, brows pinching together in concern. "Something more happened last night, didn't it?"

I hesitate, then nod. No point hiding it from her—she'll get the truth out of me one way or another.

Trina's eyes narrow. "I knew there was something you weren't saying. I felt it in my gut. Did that bastard do something to hurt you? Because if he did, I swear to God—"

"No, no, it's nothing like that," I say hastily. I take a deep breath and admit, "The job is live-in. I'd have to move in with Blaine." I swallow. "Today."

"What?" Trina stares at me, stunned. "You're joking."

"I wish I was." I slump into a chair at the table and drop my head into my hands. "His rep sprung it on us last night. Blaine didn't even know about it. I don't know what to do, Trina."

There's a long silence. Then Trina sits across from me, her expression soft with sympathy. She reaches over and grasps my hands in her own.

"I know how much this job means to you," she says in a soothing tone. "But Tals, this is a really bad idea. You barely know this guy. He could be dangerous, for all we know." Her fingers tighten around mine. "Promise me you won't do this. It's not worth the risk."

I stare at our joined hands, a lump forming in my throat. She's right, of course. Letting a near-stranger have that kind of access to me after what I went through with Jaden...it's foolish. Reckless.

But turning the job down means sacrificing my dream. Again.

I swallow hard against the sting of tears and look up at my sister. "I'm sorry," I whisper. "I can't make that promise."

"Of course, you can," Trina insists. "There'll be other opportunities, Tals"

I swallow once more. "Tri, I already signed the contract."

Trina jerks her hands away as if I've burned her. "Are you fucking kidding me?" she demands, eyes flashing. "Tell me you're kidding."

I shake my head, meeting her eyes with a pleading gaze.

Trina's eyes grow wide. "After everything you survived with Jaden, you're really going to move in with some random guy you barely know?"

"Blaine isn't like Jaden," I insist, though the words ring hollow even to me. How can I really know that after one night?

"You have no idea what he's like! You spend one night with the guy and suddenly you have a degree in Dickology that confirms he's not a psycho murderer." Trina shouts. "Tals, this is crazy. Even for us. You can't do this."

"I have to." I drop my gaze, staring at the grain of the table. "This job is my dream, Trina. My chance to rebuild what I lost. If I turn it down...I don't know if I'll get another opportunity like this." I sigh. "I've had this business registered for a year Tri, and I've done nothing with it because Jaden had convinced me that I was too fucking stupid to run my own company and too fucking fat to represent anyone in the public eye. This is my chance to prove to myself that I have what it takes to achieve my dreams. This job, this account is the first step."

"You know nothing that asshat said about you was true. Your safety is more important than a job." Trina's voice softens as she reaches for my hand again. "Please, Tals. Don't do this. You've only just started acting like yourself again after all the emotional abuse and manipulation Jaden put you through. Don't put yourself in danger again."

Her touch fills me with warmth, and the tears I've been fighting slip free. I cling to her hand like a lifeline, blinking up at her through a veil of tears.

"I'm scared," I whisper. "What if you're right? What if he..." I can't bring myself to say the words. "But I want this so badly. I don't know what to do."

Trina slides closer beside me and pulls me into her arms. I melt against her, breathing in her familiar scent.

"I'm here for you no matter what," she murmurs, stroking my

hair. "But please, promise me you'll put your safety first this time. Don't move in with him. It's too dangerous."

I close my eyes, torn between my dream and my fear. Caught between risk and regret. Sure, Blaine needs my help, regardless of whether he wants it or not. But I had agreed to do this last night more for me than him. Deep in my gut I know it's time to take a chance on myself and while I mute my gut instincts a lot, it's never led me wrong. And right now, it's telling me to take the leap.

I pull back and wipe my eyes, sniffling. "I know you worry about me. But no matter how many times I play the possible scenarios of this opportunity in my mind it ends in me still accepting it. I can't pass up this opportunity, Tri. Not again. I need to do this. Not for Jaden. Not for Blaine. For once, I'm making a decision for what will give the best benefit to me."

Trina's lips press into a thin line before sighing. "Then at least promise me you'll take precautions. Check in with me every day. And the second you feel unsafe, you get out of there."

I smile.

"I promise," I say, squeezing her hands. "You know I would never do anything to drive you nuts. You can't get rid of me from your life that easily."

"You say that, yet here we are." Her attempt at humor falls flat, edged with bitterness. I can't blame her. If our positions were reversed, I'd feel the same.

"I'm sorry," I whisper. "I never meant for any of this to happen. I honestly didn't know going in."

"I know." She pulls me close again. "Just come back to me in one piece, okay?"

I cling to her, breathing in her scent. My anchor in a sea of uncertainty. "I will. I promise."

When at last we part, an ache settles in my chest. Tomorrow I'll wake up in a strange bed, in a strange room. Without her.

I push the thought away and summon a smile. "I have a big day ahead."

Trina rolls her eyes, but I see the worry lingering behind her gaze. "You better call me the second you're settled in."

"Yes, Mother." I laugh, nudging her with my hip. The ache in my chest lessens at her answering smile.

Whatever comes next, we'll face it together. We always have.

As I pack the last of my things and glance around the apartment one final time. So many memories live within these walls. Laughter and tears, joy and heartbreak. This place has been my sanctuary for as long as I can remember. Leaving it behind feels like losing an old friend.

But I have to do this. For myself, and though it doesn't feel like it now, for Trina.

With a heavy sigh, I zip up my suitcase and roll it out into the hall. The old floorboards creak under my feet, as if saying goodbye. I pause in the doorway, gripping the handle of my suitcase until my fingernails are near piercing my palm.

You can do this, I tell myself. Stay strong. Stay determined.

I step outside and lock the door behind me, nodding to the driver Trixton had sent to take me to Blaine's.

The ride to Blaine's house seems to pass in a blur. My heart pounds as the driver helps me unload my things, and I stand gazing up at the sleek exterior in the lavish gated neighborhood.

This is really happening. I'm really doing this.

I take a deep breath and cross the garden to the front door, noticing the curious glances of the neighbors out on their verandahs. They're probably wondering who the new girl is with her mismatched luggage and nervous expression.

If only they knew the truth.

The door opens and I cross the threshold, memories of me rushing out in the wee hours of the morning fill my mind. The driver deposits my bags behind me then assures me with a smile that Blaine will be down shortly. He then abandons me, closing the door behind him.

Sighing, I look around. I hadn't stopped to get a good look at the lower floor earlier but it's gorgeous. There is beautiful wooden flooring, a fireplace, exotic furniture, a pool table and what looks to be a swimming pool beyond the side doors. I catch a glimpse of my reflection in the full-sized mirror Blaine has next to the stairwell. I hardly recognize the woman staring back at me. She looks small and afraid, a far cry from the confident business-woman I aim to be.

"You can do this," I remind my reflection.

Stay strong. Stay determined.

Trixton descends the stairs to meet me with Blaine following reluctantly behind him.

Here goes nothing.

CHAPTER 5

I glare at the sleek black town car pulling away from my driveway through my bedroom window, my jaw clenched. Trixton assured me 'Ms. Brown' was the best PR representative money could buy, but I didn't hire her. I don't need a babysitter.

But I do need this job, so I go along with the idiocrasies placed before me. Trixton, while a pain in my ass, is damn good at his job. And I need an agent so that I can keep landing these pathetic gigs to keep my mother off the streets and away from me or worse Blair.

Reluctantly, I make my way down the stairwell behind Trixton. A curvy leg along the split of a modest gray skirt catches my attention first, followed by the glorious hips that I'd knelt between only two nights ago. Then comes the rest of her—Latalia Brown. Our gazes lock as I step off the staircase.

Fuck, she's trouble.

Her full lips are coated in a luxurious maroon, her brown eyes are hooded with thick lashes, and her top shows enough cleavage to tempt a saint.

"Mr. Dixon." Her voice is like honey, thick and sweet. "Always a pleasure seeing you."

I nod but don't speak. I refuse to allow her to get to me. My plan is to play this smart. I may not be able to refuse her arrival, but I also can't be blamed if she somehow decides to leave of her own free will. There is too much at stake.

She glides toward me, her hips swaying, and extends her hand. I take it, memories of how soft her skin is rushing back to me. Her grip is firm and confident. A jolt of heat races up my arm, and I drop her hand.

Trixton for the second time in 24 hours pulls her into a hug, oblivious as always. An unwarranted pang of possessiveness rushes through me at their contact but I steady my nerves.

"Latalia, so wonderful seeing you again." He air-kisses her cheeks. "Blaine, isn't she marvelous? I gave her a virtual tour of her room, office and personal library. And she's already making notes on your schedule. Aren't you, dear?"

"Of course." Her gaze holds a challenge as she smiles at me. "I'm here to make sure Mr. Dixon's needs are met so he can focus on his work."

Needs.

I clench my jaw harder, torn between annoyance at her presumption and intrigue at her boldness. I can't remember the last time a woman looked at me like that.

"Come along then." I stride back up the grand staircase to the second floor, acutely aware of Latalia behind me. "Let's get the rest of the tour over with so we can discuss my schedule."

I'm in trouble here. Deep, deep trouble.

Her "personal library" and "office space" is really just one large room with floor-to-ceiling bookshelves, a desk, a sofa, and chairs grouped around the fireplace.

Latalia walks over to examine the leather-bound first

editions. "Dickens, Austen, the Brontës—a reader after my own heart." She smiles at me over her shoulder, eyes glowing with delight behind her glasses.

"Those were my mother's." I fold my arms, leaning against the doorframe. "I don't read fiction."

Her brows lift in surprise. "No? What do you read then?"

"Biographies. Nonfiction. Anything useful."

She tilts her head, studying me. "Reading fiction can be useful too. It fosters empathy, exposes you to new ideas and different perspectives."

"Spare me the lecture." I tap my foot, impatience simmering. "Did Trixton not explain you're here as my PR rep, not my teacher?"

Her eyes lower, but she holds my gaze. "My apologies, Mr. Dixon. As your PR rep, I'll keep your preferences in mind and not overstep in the future." Her tone is clipped, formal—and slightly wounded.

Guilt pinches me, but I shove it aside. I didn't ask for her opinions or hurt feelings.

"Excellent. If there aren't any further questions, you should get settled in. We'll go over my ground rules in an hour." I stride out, leaving Latalia and Trixton behind.

I hear Trixton apologizing before saying his goodbyes as I turn to leave. This is going to be a long transition.

An hour later, I find Latalia on my pool deck, reviewing the details of my schedule on her laptop. She glances up as I enter, her expression guarded. "Mr. Dixon. Did you want to go over today's schedule now?"

"In a minute." I cross to the bar cart at the far end of her lounge chair and pour myself a glass of bourbon. "First, there are a few ground rules we should establish."

Her spine straightens. "Of course."

I take a sip of bourbon, considering her. She's changed, dressed professionally in slacks and a blouse, hair, for the second time, has been tamed pulled back in a bun, but I can still remember the lush curves hidden beneath.

"While you're staying here, I expect discretion and professionalism at all times. No gossiping to the press or sharing details about my personal life."

Her eyes start to roll then flip closed before she responds. "Dealing with the press is a part of my job description." She pauses to release a breath. "But I can give you my word to run the statements by you prior to release." She folds her hands in her lap. "Rest assured, I take all of my client's privacy very seriously."

"Good." I set down my glass. "You'll also need to be flexible. My schedule can change on short notice, and I'll expect you to accommodate that."

"I understand completely." She nods. "Being here for your best interest, your needs and commitments will be my top priority."

"And if I have guests over who may post about me on social media, you'll need to be available whenever I require your assistance. Day or night." I hold her gaze, watching for her reaction. "Does that work with your schedule?"

I'm pushing it. But again, she is here by choice and against my preferences. She hesitates, chewing on her bottom lip. For a moment, I think she'll refuse, but then she takes a deep breath, salt lacing her tone when she responds, "Of course, Mr. Dixon. I'm here to support you however you need."

Satisfaction curls through me as I finish my bourbon. Latalia might have her own opinions, but she'll do as she's told.

"Excellent," I say, turning towards the door. "Be ready in two hours. We have dinner with my brother."

Latalia's eyebrows shoot up, her mouth opening to comment before quickly closing it again.

"You didn't mention that in the schedule you gave Trixton to share with me," she says after a beat.

I exaggerated a mock shrug before turning away to hide my smile.

"Must have slipped my mind," I confirm, sarcasm swimming around my tone. "Two hours."

A faint hint of red colors Latalia's whole face when I glance over at her, but she regains her composure in record speed.

"Understood," she replies through gritted teeth.

Stepping through the door, I begin my race against the clock. I make a mad dash to order dinner from the local barbecue buffet, hoping like hell the food would get here in time. After placing the order, I head to message Blair. It would've been faster to call but the last thing I need is Latalia passing by and figuring out that I'm drawing these dinner plans out my ass. So, text it is.

Me:

Fancy a free meal at my place?

Blair:

As in a meal you're cooking? Sorry bro, I'm not ready to meet my maker yet. Try me again another time.

I shake my head. Blair may share my face, but our personalities are vastly different, which is probably why we got along so well over the years. He's been the one constant in my ever-changing world, and unlike me, he does not mince his words. Especially when it comes to making the shortcomings of living with me very clear. And in order to make sure Latalia quits in record time, I'm going to need his quick wit. Even if it's at my own expense.

Me:

Ha ha dumb ass. There are many easier ways to off you than me

*slaving over a stove. I'm getting food from the buffet you like. Dinner
will be at six. It would really help me out if you could swing by.*

Blair:
Well since you asked so nicely. I'll see you in a bit.

When Blair strides in through the front door, I shoot him my signature smirk. His nonchalance is already apparent as he takes in the preset dining table.

Blair meets me with raised eyebrows. "So, what's the deal with dinner tonight?"

"No deals," I reply, gesturing to the place I'd set for him at the dining table. "I just thought we ought to catch up."

He grins. "Right...Catch up, sure. Because all this," he glances at the table, "fanciness isn't suspicious at all."

"Just take a seat, would ya?"

I take a swig of my bourbon to calm my nerves — not that there really was any reason to feel nervous around Blair. No matter how much we bicker and joke around, my twin brother always manages to lighten the mood. Which is his sole purpose here tonight.

Latalia walks in, her kinky hair a poof of clouds around her shoulders. She wears a dark dress that clings to her in all the right places, setting off her caramel skin. I feel a stab of desire, despite my best intentions.

She hesitates for a moment as our eyes meet but recovers swiftly, pasting on a tight-lipped smile.

"Blair, it's nice to see you again," she says, venturing further into the room.

He blinks, taking in her presence before masking his confusion with a smirk. His gaze on her irks me, but I bite it down. This is all a part of the plan. I know Blair. He'll have Latalia feeling uncomfortable staying here in no time.

"Latalia? What the hell are you doing here?" Blair asks.

"I'm Blaine's new PR representative," she answers, keeping her voice steady. "His management thought it best he moved to a live-in arrangement to accommodate his busy schedule."

Blair chuckles, tossing back his drink before glancing in my direction. "Is that so?"

I glare at him.

"So, you're his 'too hot to handle' baby sister?" Blair asks with a sleazy smile.

What the fuck is he doing?

I did not take him here to flirt with Latalia. I take a warning step toward him but Latalia crosses in front of me to close the space between them.

"Indeed," she replies, her composure unflappable. "Now, shall we eat?"

"Yes," I respond in a clipped tone. "Let's."

I meet Blair's eyes with a warning look but the ass smirks back at me in return."

The meal passes in tense silence, interrupted only by Blair's sporadic chuckles and spiteful jibes ringing through the air.

"Did you know our good boy here thinks that his 'stuffy' lifestyle is so much better than ours," Blair jeered, nudging Latalia with a wink.

Latalia takes a sip of her white wine before responding. "Does he?"

Blair stifles a laugh and I fight the urge to roll my eyes. He tells this stupid theory to almost everyone we meet.

"One thousand percent," Blair answers. "That's the sole reason he goes out of his way to maintain this massive house so close to the projects. 'Maintain' being used very loosely." He brings his hand to his chest in an exaggerated fashion. "Thank God, for his staff. Heaven knows our Blainey boy here does not have a clean bone in his body."

I clear my throat and take a sip of bourbon.

Blair smiles. "Anyway, I got off track. But yeah, he totally wants to 'enjoy' the luxuries that come with the 'celebrity life' but he can't go too far from the projects as he can't survive without my irresistible charm."

That makes Latalia laugh but she doesn't respond.

I shake my head. "You hit the nail right on the head," I tease. "Every decision I make is only for you."

To be fair Blair's theory wasn't far from the truth. I chose to buy this house as it gave me the opportunity to remain close to Blair and our mother. But the size of the house was merely a beneficial side effect.

Blair's gaze settles on Latalia, his face softening a bit. "I saw Jaden last week at the club."

Again, I clear my throat in a warning to Blair to thread lightly.

There's a pause, and I glance at Latalia. Her face is unreadable, but her posture tightens. Jaden, her ex-boyfriend, was far from a shining character in her life based on what she told me before we hooked up. Blair has been friends with Jaden for a while now but that didn't mean he supported his actions.

Latalia takes a deep breath and, when she speaks, her voice is calm and even. "I hope he's doing well."

Blair shrugs, his easy smile never leaving his face. "He's doing Jaden things. Charming every skirt in sight and running his daddy's business into the ground. The usual."

My grip tightens around my snifter.

Latalia's lips press into a thin line, but she doesn't react beyond that. Instead, she lifts her glass of wine to her lips, takes a sip, and changes the topic. It's a subtle move, but one that doesn't escape my notice. Maybe I'm being too hard on her. For all I know she's dealing with her shit. She is a mystery, and my curiosity about her grows with each passing minute.

My brother continues on with his stories, unabashed and free. Despite his occasional off-color remarks, he manages to keep the atmosphere light. Latalia's mood has clearly shifted but holds her own. She maintains her solid professional demeanor. Together, they have an interesting dynamic. I have to admit; my plan is going better than expected, and I'm enjoying their interaction more than I should.

Blair's laughter dies down, and he turns to Latalia with a smug grin. "Hey, why did you ever allow Jaden —"

"No," I interject, a warning in my voice. He's going too far, and I won't allow it. "Blair, enough."

Latalia's eyes meet mine as she sighs but remains silent.

Blair throws his hands up then grins, not the least bit phased. "Alright, alright," he says in mock surrender. "No need to get your knickers in a twist. We're just talking."

Turning to Latalia, I hope she sees the sincerity in my eyes.

"I apologize if this nincompoop is offending you," I say, unsure of why I'm backtracking on my plan.

This was the plan. *Wasn't it?*

Latalia smiles, her eyes soft. "It's alright, Blaine. I've dealt with worse."

I nod, unsatisfied. I can't allow myself to feel more than professional respect for her, but for some reason, I want to comfort her in this moment. I don't though, Instead, I return to my meal.

A comfortable silence falls over us for the rest of the meal until Blair rises with a yawn, making up some excuse to leave. Latalia also excuses herself, leaving me alone with my jacked-up thoughts. I want to be upset with Latalia. She used me. She agreed to practically be my fucking babysitter after I explicitly asked her not to. She infuriates in … but in the best ways possible.

Maybe, just maybe —

What the fuck am I saying? Shaking my head to clear my thoughts, I stand to clear the table.

I need to stick to the plan. Latalia is not interested in me the way I am her. My first impression of her was wrong. She showed me who she really was when she fucked me then snuck out.

My top priority remains to make her so uncomfortable living here she quits.

Any sexual pull I feel has to stay in my fantasies. A string of memories from my fantasies last night flash before my mind, and a groan escapes my lips. I'm playing a dangerous game, and I'm not sure I can win.

But then again, when it comes to Latalia, maybe losing wouldn't be so bad.

CHAPTER 6

LATALIA

I roll out of bed and groan as my phone's alarm blare through the room. I have been doing these therapy sessions weekly since breaking up with Jaden. And though therapy has been a staple in my whole adult life, the need for weekly sessions has become extremely helpful in the past few months. Especially with nights like last night.

The morning sun assaults me as I pull open the beige curtains to set up for my Zoom call with Dr. Reid. Yawning, I blink at the unfamiliar room around me. The entire space is a sea of muted colors and sadness, just like it's owner.

Sighing I dial in to my session.

"Good morning, Latalia," Dr Reid greets me as I enter.

It never seizes to amaze me how she can always be in such a chirpy mood at the butt crack of dawn.

"Hey doc."

"So how are we doing today?" Dr. Reid asks.

I sigh. Every session started off with the same question. It was simple. Routine. Yet today, it struck me like a ton of bricks.

"I don't know," I say, honestly. "I'm alive. So, I guess that means I should be okay. But, if I'm honest, I feel like I'm drowning in all that life is throwing my way. And though I'm clutching at my life raft, the waves just keep growing in strength."

"Okay," Dr. Reid says, her tone growing more solemn. "What do you think brought you to the sea you find yourself drowning in."

Sighing, I recount all the details of the past few days to Dr. Reid. From me quitting my job, to my one-night stand with Blaine, to me taking him on as a client, me moving in with him and finally all the things that were said at last night's dinner. Dr. Reid listens without interrupting me, making notes as needed.

"It's just a lot," I end, before taking a calming breath.

"That's definitely a lot for one week," Dr. Reid agrees. "So, if all that is what you believe brought you to the sea, you're in, what is that has grown in intensity and left you drowning?"

I swallow. The answer to that question is one I'm not certain I'm ready for.

"Blaine," I say, the word barely audible.

"Your client," Dr Reid asks.

I nod. "I know. I know you're probably thinking I'm stupid to even think there could be a chance of anything more than a fling between someone like me and someone like Blaine. And he's my client, and I have my rules. But there's just something in the way I feel when he's around me or when our eyes meet. I know this all must sound crazy. God, you must think I'm crazy."

Dr. Reid shakes her head. "I don't think you're crazy Latalia. I think you have been through traumatic things from so many of the men in your life that letting in someone new can be scary. That doesn't make you crazy. If anything, it makes you human."

I sigh. Things with Jaden had progressively deteriorated in the year we dated. But I'd been so caught up in the fact that he'd wanted to give someone who looked like me nice things in the beginning that I had missed all the red flags. And before long he had turned me against my sister, convinced me that my friends were out to get me and that my weight dictated everything I was and not allowed to do in my life.

"How can I be sure I'm not just walking back into the same patterns I did with Jaden?" I ask.

"You can't," Dr. Reid says. "But you can use the lessons learnt from your past experiences to guide your relationships in the future. The effect of those experiences can either be freeing or crippling. Only you can decide which one they'll be for you. "

My phone beeps with a reminder to meet Kamilla and Natasha at the gym in 30 minutes and I smile, happy to get out of the house and clear my head.

"That's all we have time for in today's session," Dr. Reid continues. "But feel free to call into my office should you feel we need to reconnect ahead of next week's session."

I nod, forcing a wider smile. "Thanks, Dr. Reid."

I end the call, and head into the ensuite bathroom to freshen up. With any luck, I'll be able to get all the way out the house and clear my thoughts before running into Blaine. Once ready, I creep towards the door and slowly turn the knob, peeking out into the hall. The coast is clear. As I tiptoe down the stairs, a floorboard creak behind me. I freeze in my tracks, my heart pounding.

"What on earth are you doing?" Blaine's deep, raspy voice sends a shiver down my spine. I take a deep breath and turn to face him, my cheeks burning. He stands, leaning on the frame of his bedroom door at the top of the stairs, shirtless, wearing only a pair of gray sweatpants that hang low on his hips.

I swallow hard, dragging my gaze up to his face. His lips quirk into a knowing smile and he crosses his arms, showing off his sculpted biceps.

Damn, he's fine.

"I, uh, have plans to meet some friends at the gym." I gesture at the front door behind me.

He arches a brow but doesn't press. "The gym huh?" He descends the stairs, his eyes never leaving mine. My heart all but jumps out of my chest as he stops in front of me, our bodies inches apart. "That would be good for you."

Everything in me screeches to a halt. "Excuse me?"

Blaine's face goes pale. "Fuck. No. I promise you that came out wrong." He shakes his head, his words tumbling over each other. "I mean, I do think its good you're going to the gym. But not because of how you look or anything like that." His Adam's apple bobs. "I think you're beautiful," he says softly. "I just think it's good you're not going to be cooped up in the house all by yourself when I'm gone is all."

Before I can respond, he brushes a stray curl behind my ear and cups my cheek. I gasp at his touch, heat flooding my veins. Our eyes lock and the air between us shifts.

I clear my throat and take a step back, breaking the spell. "I should get going."

Blaine's hand falls away, but his gaze remains intense. "Have fun with your friends."

I nod and turn to leave before I do something I'll regret, like throw myself into his arms... again. As I walk to my car, I take deep breaths of the crisp morning air, trying to calm my racing pulse.

God, I need to clear my head.

By the time I arrive at the gym, I've convinced myself that moment with Blaine was a fluke. An aberration that can't...won't happen again. I spot Kamilla and Natasha waiting for me by the front entrance and paste a smile on my face as I join them.

"You're late," Kamilla says, giving me a knowing look. "Hot night with Mr. Hotness?"

"No. And my 'client' has a name." I roll my eyes before looping my arm through hers as we head inside. "So, what's the plan for today?"

Natasha shoots Kamilla a look before linking her arm with mine. "Girl, I know you lying and as smooth as that subject change attempt us, we're not buying it."

We walk hand in hand over to the ellipticals and hop on with the girls on either side of me.

Kamilla glances over to me. "Now spill."

I hesitate, searching for the right words.

With a sigh, I say, "Blaine paid me a compliment this morning."

"And?" Natasha prompts.

"And nothing. He said he thought I was beautiful and told me to have fun with my friends, I thanked him, end of story."

Kamilla snorts. "Yeah, right. I can see it in your eyes, girl. There's more to it than that."

I drop my gaze to the floor. She's right, of course. There's so much more. Feelings I don't want or plan to acknowledge.

"Did he finally make a move?" Natasha asks. "Tell me you guys kissed again or something."

"No!" My face flames at the thought. "Nothing like that happened. Blaine is now just a client, remember? I would never cross that line."

"But you want to." Kamilla's knowing tone makes it a statement rather than a question.

I don't bother denying it. My friends can see right through me. "It doesn't matter what I want," I say. "Blaine is now off-limits. End of story."

"Right, because of your rules?" Natasha asks. "Or because you're afraid?"

I bristle at the question. "I'm not afraid. I'm being professional. Blaine pays me to do a job, and that's all this is. All I plan to have it be."

"Keep telling yourself that." Kamilla pats my arm. "Sooner or later, you'll have to admit the truth."

I glance over at Kamilla. "Right, like you admit that you'd have Jackson banging you senseless every night instead of some new bimbo."

Kamilla lowers her eyes in my direction.

"Don't you turn this around on me." Kamilla quips back, blushing. "Jackson is just my roommate."

"Yeah, a very sexy roommate that you wanna break your own rules for," Natasha adds, making us all laugh.

Jackson has been Kamilla's roommate for about two years now and though she will never admit it, we all feel the sexual tension between them whenever he's around. So, it's real rich for her to be the one teasing me about denying my feelings for a guy.

"I can't stand y'all," Kamilla teases, in between bouts of laughter.

"Bitch please," Natasha teases. "You know you can't live without us."

We all laugh.

"No lies told," I add, between laughter.

"I didn't say I didn't love y'all," Kamilla clarifies. "It doesn't mean I gotta like y'all right now."

We all laugh again.

"Ten minutes of weights?" I ask hopping off the elliptical to head to the Lat station.

Both girls nod and follow suit.

"Damn girl, don't you hear the machine crying under all that weight?" A meaty guy walking by asks, snorting. "Why don't you hop off and give the machine to someone who actually cares about how they look."

My face flames as embarrassment washes over me. I open my mouth, but no sound comes out. I don't know this jerk, but his cruel words cut deep.

Before I can respond, Kamilla is in his face, eyes blazing. "What did you just say asshole?" Her voice is low and dangerous.

The guy smirks. "You heard me. Just telling her the truth. She should stick to the elliptical or the weight loss surgeries so she can look less like an eye sore and maybe get a man."

"The only truth here is that you're a pathetic excuse for a human being," Kamilla snarls. "Latalia is strong, brave and beautiful. She doesn't need to change a thing to attract someone with an ounce of decency or intelligence. Unlike you."

"Whatever," the guy mutters. "Keep lying to the fat cow if you want."

"What the fuck is your problem?" I ask, Natasha and I joining Kamilla in front of the man. The three of us, of course, are no match for him but all willing to get beaten trying.

Kamilla lifts her chin, radiating rage. "Get the fuck out of here before we have you banned from this gym. And take your toxic attitude with you."

The man glares at us before stalking off, and Kamilla turns to me, her expression softening. "Don't listen to idiots like that. You're amazing just the way you are."

Tears prick my eyes as I pull them both into a hug. "Thank you for standing up for me," I whisper.

"That's what friends are for." They hug me back.

"What do you say we head out," Natasha suggests.

"Yeah, the aura here got stank real quick," I add.

Kamilla nods and we head off to the locker room.

CHAPTER 7

The Calvin Sparrow studio is cold and sterile, all sharp edges and glossy white floors. I sit in an uncomfortable metal chair, resisting the urge to fidget. Trixton paces in front of me, pale hands fluttering as he speaks.

"This could be huge for you, Blaine. Calvin Sparrow wants exotic, and you've got that in spades." He shoots me a pointed look, gaze flickering to the scar beneath my right eye. I grit my teeth, fist clenching in my lap.

After five years in this business, you'd think I'd be used to it. The lingering stares, the assumptions. But it still makes my skin crawl. I'm more than a few scars and a six-pack. I have a degree in business, for fuck's sake. But none of that matters here.

I take a deep breath and force a smile. "You really think I have a shot at this?"

Trixton beams, clasping his hands together. "Absolutely. And if it goes well, there's talk of a movie role. A lead role." He pauses, eyes glinting. "But you need to clean your public image clean and nail this audition. You need to smolder, give them intensity. Make them forget you're even wearing clothes."

I swallow hard, jaw clenching. Of course. What else is new?

Trixton's gaze turns sympathetic. "I know it's not ideal. But this could open so many doors, Blaine. Think of the opportunities."

Opportunities. That's how he always convinces me, dangling success just out of reach like a carrot on a string. I sigh, resignation settling in my bones. "Alright. I'll do my best."

Trixton grins, clapping his hands together. "Excellent! You're on next.

I clear my throat, shifting in my seat. "There's something else."

Trixton arches a brow, gaze sharpening. "Yes?"

"Latalia. She doesn't need to be staying with me." I pause, searching for the right words. "Don't get me wrong, I sure she's brilliant at her job. But I don't need a babysitter. I'll do just fine without her."

Plus, if I don't get her out of my air soon, I'm going to end up with her in my bed. I think to myself but refrain from saying.

"Is that so?" Trixton asks coolly.

I frown at his tone. "Come on, you know it's true. The media has moved on. Latalia and I don't need to live or work together. It's time she goes back to her place."

"I disagree." Trixton sits across from me and folds his hands against his chest, eyes hard. "You may think your reputation has recovered, but the public is fickle. One wrong move and we're back to square one." He leans forward, gaze piercing. "Latalia stays. Her reputation in the industry is the only reason Calvin Sparrow is even a thing. So, you'll keep her around for as long as we see fit. Understand?"

Anger flares in my chest, hot and sharp. I hate being told what to do, especially with my own damn life. But one look at Trixton's expression and I bite my tongue. Trixton was the only agent willing to even touch me with a ten-foot pole when I was just starting out in the industry. And now that the tabloids have deemed me the problematic black man in the industry no other agents are going to give me the time of day if Trixton drops me. So, I need to play by his rules, at least for now.

I swallow, fingers curling into fists. "Fine. But I'm not going to pretend we're something we're not. Latalia and I are going to have to agree to stay on our own sides of the house. We're not friends, and we're sure as hell not playing house."

"I don't care what arrangements you make, as long as she's allowed to continue working her miracles." Trixton shrugs, dismissing me. "Now, how about you go kill that audition."

I tune him out, staring out the window with a scowl.

The audition goes off without a hitch. My mind stuck on thoughts of Latalia and how on earth I'm going to get through the next how ever long she'll be living in my house without claiming her body and soul.

An hour later, I walk through the front door of my house, sighing when I see Latalia standing out on the pool deck. My plan had been to head down to my home gym once I got home, but for some odd reason my feet moved toward the sliding door leading to the pool instead of down to the basement.

Latalia turns as I step onto the deck. The corners of my mouth twitch upwards. "Blaine, sorry I didn't hear you come in." She brushes her hands over her sweats. "I'll head back up to my room."

I arch a brow. "Do I make you uncomfortable?" I ask, a light hint of concern in my tone.

"No. I just didn't come here to play games," she retorts, finally managing to keep her eyes from wandering. There's an edge to her voice, but a light flush still lingers in her cheeks, making it hard for me to take her stern look seriously.

"And something about my demeanor screams player to you?" I challenge, a single brow arching.

She sighs. "I just want us to clear the air," she says, voice steady despite the color on her cheeks. "Get the elephant out the room."

I move toward the mini bar by the pool deck. "Fine. What can I get you?" I ask, glancing over my shoulder. She's looking at me again, but this time her eyes are on my face, lips pursed.

"Water's fine," she replies, her gaze steady. I fill a glass and hand it to her, our fingers brushing in the exchange. A jolt of heat rushes through me at the contact, but I ignore it, focusing instead on the cool condensation on the glass.

"Alright, Latalia. You have my attention." I say, leaning against the counter, arms crossed over my chest. "What's on your mind?"

She takes a deep breath. "I know me walking out on you the other day made you upset. And though I still don't fully understand why you wanted me to stay in the first place, I'm sorry if me leaving like that offended you in any way. I promise it was more about me protecting myself than hurting you." She takes a gulp of her water. "Now that I got that out. I hope we can put the past behind us, and you'll give this arrangement a genuine shot as I may not be good at a lot of things, but I'm great at my job. And I can get your image to where it needs to be."

I study her for a moment, appreciating her professionalism. Even with all our tension, she stays focused on the task at hand. It's admirable. Annoying, considering the only thing running through my mind at the moment is capturing those plump lips of hers with my own, but admirable.

"I can admit the way I handled that whole situation wasn't my best hour." I sigh. "If I'm honest, there are imperfections that I have that make me feel like an outcast in the superficial industry that I'm in. So, when people walk out on me like that, I guess it sends me to a bad place. Anyway. Thank you for the apology." I push off the counter to pace the deck. "Apparently, everyone seems to believe that having you here is 'good for me', so I'll have to concede. But I don't have to pretend to like it."

She nods, taking another sip of her water. "I understand. I'll do my best to give you your space."

"Perfect. Stay on your side of the house and I'll stay on mine, outside of the common areas," I propose. "And we can remain professional, forget about whatever happened between us in the past. Agreed?"

"Agreed," she says, extending her hand. I take it, and her grip is firm, the contact sparking that familiar heat I can't shake between us.

"Good," I say, tearing my hand away from her grip. "Now, I have an important call planned any minute so I'm going to enjoy what's left of the sunshine before I'm summoned. I'll be out here if you need anything," I say, dismissing her with a wave of my hand.

Latalia nods and heads inside, leaving me alone. I strip off my shirt and jeans, settling into a lounge chair in just my boxers. The heat of the sun soaks into my skin as I close my eyes, my muscles unwinding.

A throat clears nearby, and I crack open an eye to find Latalia hovering by the patio doors. "Did you need something?"

"Yes, actually. I just wanted to say I know you felt some kind of way about me leaving the other day." She won't meet my gaze, her fingers fidgeting by your side as she stares at the tile floor. "But it had nothing to do with you or your performance that night," she continues, eyes locking on the growing bulge in my boxers. "You were actually pretty great." She clears her throat. "Anyway, I guess I just wanted to say talking for giving this work relationship a chance. I'll be in my office if you need anything." She stops talking but she doesn't move.

Amusement rises in my chest. I hadn't been expecting an apology after her whole performance last night. And while I know the correct response is something heart felt. But the fact that she's still ogling my cock makes it real difficult to not continue my bratty act.

"See something you like?" I tease.

Her eyes fly to mine, embarrassment etched across her face. She opens and closes her mouth, but no sound comes out. Delighted by her reaction, I arch a brow and watch her squirm.

Finally, finding her voice, she flips back into work mode. "I apologize for interrupting you, Mr. Dixon. It won't happen again."

She disappears into the house so quickly a dark curl bounces out her bun. Chuckling under my breath, I settle back into the lounge chair, enjoying the warmth of the sun on my skin. Latalia's going to be far more entertaining than I expected.

An hour passes in peaceful solitude before the patio doors slide open again. I don't bother opening my eyes this time, assuming Latalia needs something. The scent of coconut sunscreen wafts over me as footsteps pad across the tiles.

A shadow falls across my face, and I crack an eye open to find Latalia hovering beside me once more, now dressed in a modest turquoise bikini. My gaze roams over her lush curves before meeting her wary expression. All the memories of my hands and mouth dancing over her bare skin rush back to my mind and I swallow a groan.

"Can I help you with something?" I manage to get out, my voice breathier than intended.

She presses her lips together, unease flickering in her eyes. "I thought I should inform you I'll be using the pool for some exercise. I didn't want you to be startled if you saw me."

A smile tugs at the corners of my lips. She's trying to avoid another embarrassing encounter, though she clearly has no idea how seeing her in that bikini affects me. Heat pools in my groin, and I adjust myself discreetly.

"Thanks for the heads up," I say, keeping my tone light. Her gaze darts to my crotch for a split second before she looks away, color flooding her cheeks. A smirk tugs at my mouth as I close my eyes again. "Enjoy your swim."

I listen as she arranges her things on a lounge chair and slides into the water. The sounds of splashing and her occasional sighs filter over me, causing arousal to simmer in my veins. It's going to take all my restraint not to join her, to run my hands over her wet skin and taste the droplets on her lips. I bury my face in the crook of my arm with a groan, my cock throbbing. Maintaining my professionalism around Latalia is going to be far more difficult than I anticipated.

The splashing stops, and I open my eyes to find Latalia gazing at me from the pool, cheeks flushed, and lips parted. Her nipples are visible through her bikini top, hardened peaks that make my mouth water. She licks her lips, and I'm done for.

I stand and stalk toward her, desire burning in my veins like lava. Her eyes widen, pupils dilating as I step into the water.

"Blaine, what are you doing?" Her voice is breathy, any protest weak.

"What I should have done from the moment I saw you last night in that damned steakhouse," I say, my tone husky.

I cup the back of her neck and crush my mouth to hers, groaning at the feel of her soft lips moving beneath mine. Her hands clench my biceps as she whimpers, the sound shooting straight to my cock. I deepen the kiss, thrusting my tongue past her lips to delve into the sweet heat of her mouth.

She moans, the vibration thrumming against my lips, and presses closer. My hands slide down to palm the generous curve of her ass, squeezing gently. I'm drowning in her, lost to the taste and feel and scent of Latalia. Nothing else matters but having her, all of her, right now.

I break the kiss to rasp, "Bedroom. Now."

Latalia nods, eyes glazed with the same ravenous need coursing through me. I lift her easily - again happy as fuck that weight added cross-fit had been my coping mechanism to deal with my mother over the years. Her legs wrap around my waist, and I carry her into the house. Our mouths clash as I make my way upstairs, stumbling once or twice in my haste.

Finally, inside her room, I set her on her feet and reach for the ties of her bikini top. "Tell me to stop, Latalia, and I will." My voice is rough with longing. "But I want this. I want you. You're fucking beautiful. Alcohol has nothing to do with it."

Her gaze locks with mine, eyes dark and hungry. "Don't stop," she whispers. "I want this too."

Triumph and lust roar through me as I strip her bare, drinking in the sight of her gorgeous body.

I lower my lips to her neck planting delicious kisses on a path to her erect nipples.

A loud roar fills the air as my phone rings out and I curse under my breath.

"Ignore it," I growl, before filling my mouth with the tip of her right breast. She whimpers as I roll my tongue over her nipple.

My phone's ringtone blares again, but I don't stop.

"You said you were expecting an important call," Latalia says, easing her breast out my mouth then stepping back. "Go."

"No," I protest.

Latalia sighs. "The reason I'm here is to ensure you are not missing important obligations, not be the cause of it." She covers her breasts. "I'm not going anywhere." She confirms as if sensing my hesitation. "Go handle your business."

My phone rings again, and I nod before answering the call and heading to my office.

CHAPTER 8

LATALIA

The door clicks shut behind Blaine, leaving me alone with my thoughts. Which isn't a good thing right now. My lips still tingle from his kisses. I press them together, trying to ignore the sensation, but that only makes it worse. I can still taste him, a mix of coffee, bourbon, and something spicy and masculine.

I groan and flop back on the bed, staring up at the ceiling.

What the hell am I doing?

I also have strict rules about getting mixed up with clients. Strict, iron-clad rules that I've already bent into pretzels.

I grab my phone, my fingers moving faster than my brain as I open the Sisterhood group chat with Natasha, Kamilla, and Trina.

Me:
SOS! Mayday! I'm failing at this whole "keep it professional" thing.

. . .

NATASHA:

Oh no, what happened?

Me:

Blaine just left. I went for a swim. Saw all his sexy man parts again and fell into a dick trance. But he came up and kissed me and bitch there were sparks ... again.

KAMILLA:

Again?! Girl, you didn't tell us about the first time!

Me:

I know, I know. I was trying to pretend it didn't happen. Blamed it on the alcohol. But I'm sober this time and the sparks were definitely still there. If his phone hadn't rung when it did, I probably would have ended up riding him into the sunset.

TRINA:

Get it, girl! You deserve some fun. Just be safe.

Me:

It's not that simple! He's a client now. I have rules about this kind of thing.

KAMILLA:

Again with the self-inflicted rules. If the chemistry is that hot, you gotta explore it!

NATASHA:

I agree. This could be the start of something amazing. Don't shut it down before it even has a chance.

Me:

But what if it ends up complicating things?

TRINA:

Life is complicated. Love even more so. You can't avoid it just because it might get messy.

Me:

I hate it when you're all reasonable and logical.

TRINA:

We aim to please. Now go get your man!

I LAUGH and set down my phone, feeling lighter than I have all day. My girls are insane, but they're right. I can't ignore this connection I have with Blaine. The complications will still be there whether I pursue something with him or not.

Maybe it's time I bend my rules a little more. After all, there isn't a rule that prevents me from creating new rules. My lips curve into a smile as I think of Blaine's kiss, and the promise of more to come.

Blaine bursts into the room, startling me from my thoughts. Panic is etched into his features.

"There's an emergency. I have to go."

I spring to my feet. "What's wrong? How can I help?"

"It's my mother. She's...not well." He runs a hand through his hair, gaze distant. "I need to get to her before she does something she regrets."

Though confused by his vague explanation, I don't press for details. His distress is clear. "I'm coming with you."

"You don't have to —"

"I'm not letting you face this alone." I throw on a dry pair of panties and a sun dress then grab my purse. "Now, where do we need to go?"

Gratitude flickers in his eyes and he squeezes my hand. "Thank you."

We hurry out to his car, and he speeds through the streets, tension radiating from him. I reach over and lace my fingers through his. He grips back like a lifeline. We arrive at a small house in a rundown neighborhood. As soon as Blaine unlocks the front door, a disheveled woman comes stumbling out.

"Blainey!" She throws her arms around him, nearly toppling them both.

The stench of alcohol and something else assaults my senses. Blaine steadies her with difficulty, a cocktail of emotions etched into his face as he looks at her.

She's high. And by Blaine's reaction, this isn't the first time.

"Blainey," his mother drawls once more. "Why won't Blair come play? I need ... I need to tell him I'm sorry. You too. I never should've made you do it. I was -"

"It's okay, ma," Blaine says, his voice shaky. "Let's just get you back, okay?" Blaine's voice cracks for a moment but he steels himself.

My heart aches for him. I know then that she's the reason for the shadows I sometimes see in his eyes. The reason he's so fiercely protective of those he cares for.

I move to help support her from the other side, giving Blaine's hand another squeeze. "I've got you," I whisper to both of them. "Everything will be okay."

He blinks back tears and nods. Together, we get his mother into the house and settled in a chair. Blaine swallows hard, his eyes shining, and for a moment I fear he might cry. But he takes a deep, steadying breath and pulls back, gaze clear once more.

"We should find my brother," he says briskly. "Before she wakes up and decides to bolt again."

I nod.

Blaine frowns. "He could be anywhere at this point. Under a bed, in the bathtub." He sighs. "I could do this part alone. It could get...ugly." He winces. "Well, uglier."

"Blaine." I cup his cheek, forcing his gaze onto mine. "I told you—you're not alone. I'm here for you, no matter what. So, stop trying to protect me and let me help, okay?"

His eyes soften, and he turns his head to press a kiss to my palm. "Okay," he says roughly. "Thank you."

"You're welcome." I squeeze his hand and move through the apartment. It's fairly big but mostly empty. There is not much furniture and just a minimal kitchen. The living room is dim and disordered, empty liquor bottles strewed about and the lingering scent of weed in the air. Blaine's jaw clenches at the state of things, but he stays focused on finding Blair.

We split up, with him getting his mother settled on the couch so she doesn't fall, and me checking one of the closets—but then a faint whimpering reaches my ears. I glance around, zeroing in on a slightly open door at the end of a short hallway. Blair's bedroom. I move toward the bedroom to investigate. Pushing open the door, my heart clenches at the sight that greets me.

Blair is huddled in the far corner of the room, rocking back and forth with his hands fisted in his hair. His eyes are wide and unseeing, lips moving in a frantic, unintelligible mantra. "No mama, not today. Not today mama"

He's lost in the throes of a panic attack. I may not know the full details of their history, but right now that's irrelevant. I hurry over to him, dropping to my knees and reaching out slowly so as not to startle him further. "Blair," I say softly, grasping one of his hands. "Blair, it's okay. We're here now."

His eyes snap to mine, still wild with panic. But he latches onto my hand like a lifeline, squeezing so hard it's nearly painful. I don't flinch, just keep murmuring reassurances as I rub his back in slow circles.

Eventually his breathing evens out and the panic starts to recede from his eyes. But his grip on my hand remains firm, as if he's afraid I'll disappear the moment he lets go.

I'm not going anywhere.

I glance over at Blaine, who's hovering nearby with a pinched, worried expression. He meets my gaze, but his expression is unreadable.

"I'll be right back okay," I say to Blair, not really wanting to leave him on his own but needing to ensure Blaine is okay.

"I'm sorry you had to see all of this —"

"Stop," I say cutting him off. "We're not doing that. Life is sometimes ugly."

Blaine drops his gaze to the floor next to his mom.

"Hey," I say, a bit more forceful than intended. "I'm here for you. Whatever you need, I got you."

"You said you were coming back," Blair calls out from the room.

I glance behind me. "I'll be right there."

Blair meets my eyes, but his mom wakes back up before he can speak.

He holds on to her before she can bolt. "I need to get her back to the hospice. But Blair needs me."

"Go," I say. "I'll stay here with Blaine.

He shakes his head. "I can't ask you to do that."

His mom wrestles her hand away from Blaine, but he grabs onto her other arm. I give him a light push.

"I'm gonna be here for you whether you fight me on this or not. But you need to take care of your mom." I lock my gaze onto his. "I'll stay with Blair. Go."

Blaine nods, mouthing a silent thank you.

Without waiting for him to leave, I turn and head back to Blair.

"Hey, you," I say, sliding back down to sit on the ground beside Blair. "Wanna talk about what's on your mind?"

He shakes his head, eyes downcast. "Not yet. Just...stay. Please."

"Of course." I scoot closer until our thighs are pressed together, a warm and comforting weight. "I'm right here."

We sit in silence for a long moment. Blair rests his head on my shoulder with a shuddering sigh, still clinging to my hand. I bring my other arm around him in a loose embrace, rubbing his back in a steady rhythm.

"She wasn't supposed to find me here," he says at last, voice rough with emotion. "Blaine said he'd taken care of her. I thought I'd finally gotten away."

My heart aches for him. No wonder the sight of his mother sent him into a tailspin; it's clear this isn't the first time she's tracked him down when he least expected it. "I'm so sorry," I murmur. "You deserve to feel safe in your own home."

"Not your fault." He tilts his head up to meet my gaze, eyes soft with gratitude. "But thank you. For this."

A lump forms in my throat at the vulnerability in his

expression. All I want is to shield him from any more pain. "You don't have to go through this alone anymore," I tell him fiercely. "I'm here for you, and so is Blaine. We've got your back."

The corners of his mouth quirk up in a tremulous smile. "Yeah?"

"Yeah." I give his hand a gentle squeeze. "I promise."

Blair exhales a long, slow breath and visibly relaxes against me. "Thank you," he says again, voice thick with emotion. "You have no idea how much that means."

I brush a kiss over his hair as my mother used to do for me. A fiercely protective surge of affection welling up inside me. "You're welcome."

We sit there together in silence for a few minutes, taking comfort in each other's presence. The tension slowly drains from Blair's body as I continue rubbing his back, his breathing evening out into something calmer and steadier.

By the time Blaine returns from taking his mother back to the hospice, Blair has drifted off to sleep in my arms. Blaine pauses in the doorway, gaze softening at the sight of us. "How is he?" he asks in a whisper.

"Better now, I think." I brush a stray lock of hair from Blair's forehead, a surge of tenderness flooding through me. "He was really shaken up, but I talked him down."

Blaine's expression gentles his eyes still glossy. "Thank you for taking care of him. I don't know how I'd have handled all this alone."

A flush of pleasure warms my cheeks at the praise. "Of course. I meant what I said—we're here for each other."

"And I can't tell you how much that means to me. Especially now that I believe it." Blaine crosses the room to kneel beside us, smoothing a hand over his brother's hair. "I gotta take care of them. They're why I do everything."

My heart swells at the raw emotion in his voice. Maybe this

thing between us is moving faster than I'm used to, but in this moment, I have no doubts.

"Let me just get him off the ground. Then we can go. Okay?"

I nod. He leans over and kisses me softly. I don't protest. Shivers run down my core, and I know it was useless fighting it anymore.

"What are you doing to me?" Blaine asks.

I think about saying something witty related to my job, but the truth falls out of my mouth. "Probably the same thing you're doing to me."

Blaine's eyes flicker up to mine, but he doesn't respond. Instead, he stands and moves to ease Blair off my shoulder so I could stand. I grab hold of Blair's left side and we move him together to the bed.

"Do you mind if I use the bathroom?" I ask. Desperate to escape the ambush of emotions and thoughts in my head.

"Sure," Blaine responds. "Down the hall, to the right."

I nod and hold my composure long enough to get out of the room. I rush to the bathroom, flinging the door closed behind me so I could reclaim the breath that Blaine stole from me with that kiss.

CHAPTER 9

BLAINE

The scent of bacon wafts under my door, rousing me from sleep. I rub the grit from my eyes and blink at the sunlight filtering through the blinds. My kitchen must be in love with Latalia as it hasn't seen this much action since I moved in. I never bothered to unpack more than the essentials. I'm hardly home anyway and I hate doing dishes, so takeout is my friend.

I roll onto my back and stare up at the ceiling. I should go out there. Attack the day and all that jazz, but the regret pooling in my gut keeps me in place. I should've opened up to Latalia last night. Deep inside, I know it would've been the right thing to do, and I had intended to initially, but after the episode with my mother, and seeing Blair move four steps back, I'd been too drained.

Something shifted between Latalia and me though, that much was clear. There was a curiosity about what might come from having her here in my space that I couldn't shake. Fuck, I'd even started envisioning her as a more stationary fixture in my life.

71

I chuckle, picturing her jumping into that sundress that clung to her curves last night. She really does care, regardless of how much she may try to hide it. But I'll continue to play along with her façade of having a steely exterior. That body of hers, though. That body is going to drive me crazy. The memory of her nipples pebbling under her dress stirs heat in my groin. I want to explore the desire she evokes, peel away her clothes and learn the slopes and swells of her body. But only if she wants me to get to know her. Because the part of her that she hides away, that's the part of her that intrigues me.

With a sigh, I drag myself from bed and pull on a pair of sweatpants, and white T-shirt. I follow the scent of breakfast down the hall, pausing in the doorway to drink in the sight of her. Latalia stands at the stove, her back to me, hips swaying to music only she can hear. She's ditched the sundress for a pair of shorts and a tank top, the hem riding up to expose the dimples at the base of her spine.

My mouth goes dry. I want to press my lips to that spot, trace the indentations with my tongue. I clench my fists, tamping down the urge. We haven't even been on a real date yet. I can't rush this.

As if sensing my gaze, Latalia glances over her shoulder. A smile blooms on her face, warmth flooding her eyes. "Morning." She flips the bacon with a fork. "Breakfast is almost ready."

"You didn't have to do this." I clear my throat, willing my body to behave.

"I wanted to. Besides..." She turns, wiping her hands on a dish towel. Her gaze drifts to my sweatpants, a blush staining her cheeks. "I figured you'd need your strength for today."

Amusement wars with arousal, heat pooling low in my abdomen. Today is shaping up to be far more interesting than I anticipated. I sidle up next to her and pluck a piece of bacon from the pan, popping it in my mouth.

"Well, in that case, you'd better feed me up." I slant her a heated look, desire kindling a spark in her eyes. "I have a feeling I'll need all the energy I can get."

She laughs, the sound husky and full of promise, and I swoon like I'm in a goddamned Hallmark movie. I'm in trouble if my plan is to keep my hands to myself until I can get to know her. Real trouble.

We settle at the table, conversation flowing easily between us as we eat. I ask about her plans for the day, her voice lulling me into a sense of comfort I rarely feel.

"I was thinking I'd tag along with you to your first shoot today to see if I could have a chat with some of the photographers and crew on set. It may be good to get fresh perspectives for the campaign I'm building." She shrugs, gazing at me through her lashes. "Before that though, I'm wide open. That is, unless you had something else in mind?"

The implication is clear. Heat coils in my abdomen at the thought of spending the morning in bed with her, learning the curves and hollows of her body until she comes apart beneath my hands and mouth.

I clear my throat, shifting in my seat.

Her laughter fills the air. "Calm down. I'm only kidding. There is a ton of things we both have to do today or Trixton will have both our heads."

"Is that so?" I tease. "So, I guess you are back in the hat of only PR rep then?" My question is both disappointment and intrigue.

"I assure you I never left my professional role," she insists. "Even if it does come in spurts as I 'enjoy' your company."

I swallow a smile. "Am I still sleeping, or did you just admit to the fact that my charm is wearing you down."

Latalia rolls her eyes while chewing her bacon.

"Someone should take you back to elementary school so they can teach you the meaning of simple words," she says behind a smile. "I'm positive we have two separate meanings of the word 'charm.'"

I wiggle my eyebrows in her direction before taking a sip of my coffee.

"Any way," Latalia continues. "There's been a few adjustments to the schedule that Trixton sent over." She pauses to wipe her hand with a piece of hand towel before pulling out her tablet. "First, there's the midday shoot that I'll be tagging along to, then you have editorial with Vybe that should take you up to about 5PM. After, we can squeeze in a quick dinner there and finally there is a one-hour therapy session that I booked for you with the amazing Dr Angela Reid at 6PM, so maybe dinner after would be better.

The mirth fades from my expression as I recall the last item on her list in my mind.

I know she did not just fucking say what I think she did.

"Did you just say therapy?" I ask, everything in me contracting as she nods.

"I don't need a shrink poking around in my head," I say, my anger seeping into my tone far quicker than I had intended.

Latalia arches a brow, undeterred. "Everyone can benefit from therapy, Blaine." She reaches a handout to rest on mine. "It will help you work through unresolved issues from your past so you can move forward in a healthy way."

And there it was. The sole reason why people barely get the privilege to see what my life was like behind the curtains. One look at what my brother and I go through with my mom, and she decides I'm a fucking lunatic.

"I'm dealing with my 'issues', as you put them just fine on my own." I jerk my hand from her grasp, irritation simmering in my veins.

"Are you?" She tilts her head, regarding me with a knowing look. "You put up a good front, I'll give you that. But I can see the cracks in your walls. Talking to someone impartial can only help."

"I don't have fucking issues," I snap, shoving away from the table. Her concern only serves to highlight my weaknesses, flaws I prefer to keep hidden. "And I sure as hell don't need some over-paid woman poking around my head to sort through problems I don't have."

I pace the length of the table, my breathing labored. Latalia remains seated as she studies me. This is the part of having people in my space that I hate. Them seeing me unbalanced, leaving me raw and exposed. I hate being vulnerable. If my mother taught me nothing else is that vulnerability is the biggest sign of weakness.

The fact that Latalia is just sitting there sipping coffee further infuriates me. After several passes, I pivot to face her.

"Well? Aren't you going to argue your point?" I fold my arms over my chest, bracing for an attack.

She shakes her head, regarding me as my mother often does when sober. As if my anger is unwarranted.

"You already know how I feel," she begins. "The decision to sign you up for therapy began being strictly about what would be best for your public image. But I'd be lying if I didn't admit that what happened last night also now plays a factor in my recommendation." She meets my eyes. "All that being said, this is still your choice, Blaine. I'll support you either way."

The fight drains from me, replaced by a bone-deep weariness. I scrub a hand over my face, exhaustion etching its way into every line of my body. Latalia pushes to her feet and closes the distance between us, wrapping me in her arms.

I tense for the briefest second before melting into her embrace. She smells of lavender and honey, a balm to my frayed nerves. I curl into her, soaking in the solace she so readily provides.

"I'm sorry," I mumble against her neck. "The idea of therapy..." I trail off with a helpless shrug.

"You have nothing to apologize for." She strokes a hand down my back, her touch soothing. "I understand this is difficult for you. And even if you opt not to go to the therapy session, you can always talk to me. About anything, anytime. I'm here to listen without judgment."

A knot forms in my throat. Outside of Blair, no one has ever offered me such unconditional support. Latalia is shaping up to be my port in the storm that has become my life. And I don't know why, but in this moment, I trust her. So, if she believes therapy will help quiet the demons hounding my every step, then I owe it to her—and myself—to try.

I tighten my arms around her waist, breathing in her scent once more. "Maybe we can try one session. See how it goes."

SHE PRESSES a kiss to my cheek, lips curving in a smile. "That's all I ask. I just want you to be at peace." Her smile gentles into something tender that makes my chest ache with emotion. "You deserve that and so much more."

I pull back to meet her gaze, struck by the depth of feeling reflected in her eyes.

"How did I ever get lucky enough to find you?" The question slips out before I can stop it.

Latalia's smile widens, crinkling the corners of her eyes. "You didn't, if I recall you didn't think you needed a babysitter, plus I don't ever remember being lost, or waiting to be found." She drags her nails down my chest, igniting sparks along every nerve ending she brushes. "But if I was to ever play away with the whole needing to be found scenario, it doesn't hurt to be found by a man who's as sexy as sin. "

Heat infuses my face at her blunt praise. I'm not accustomed to receiving compliments, not like this at least. Not from anyone that mattered. And Latalia was starting to matter.

"In that case, let me find you." I angle my head, brushing my mouth against hers. The kiss starts slow but builds in intensity.

My hands roam her body, relearning her shape, the dip of her waist, the swell of her hips.

I cup her ass and she release a soft moan as I pull her against my hardening cock. Breaking the kiss, I trail my lips along her jaw and down the column of her throat. Her pulse flutters under my tongue, beating in sync with my own racing heart.

"We have to leave soon." Her protest lacks conviction, desire evident in the husky pitch of her voice.

"We have time." I walk her backward toward the couch, reluctance slowing my steps. As much as I want her, I won't rush what's between us, not unless she wants this too. Latalia deserves better, deserves the world, and I aim to give it to her.

When the back of her knees hit the edge of the couch, she sinks down onto the cushion. A flush stains her cheeks as she gazes up at me with darkened eyes. Never have I seen a more tempting sight.

"Come here," she murmurs, crooking a finger at me.

I follow her silent command without thought, settling my body over hers. We kiss and touch, slow and deep, no destination in mind, simply enjoying the journey. My tongue explores her mouth once more. Smiling as she gives my bottom lip a light nib. I break the kiss, nudging her chin up to gain access to the delicate skin of her throat. She sighs in pleasure, the sound eliciting a groan from me as I lavish open-mouthed kisses along her pulse point.

"We should stop." Her protest lacks conviction, desire evident in the breathless quality of her voice.

"Do you want me to stop?" I lift my head, searching her face for any sign of discomfort. What I find instead is longing, a mirror of my own desire.

A coy smile plays on her lips. "No. But we have things to do today, remember?"

"I remember."

I capture her mouth again, the sweet taste of her like ambrosia on my tongue before I pull away once more.

"But its at noon, which gives me about 90 minutes until I need to leave." I kiss her again lightly. "And I do need to take a shower. A long, warm shower, preferably in your juices. As I recall you were a squirter."

She shivers beneath me, and I recapture her mouth. My hands roam her curves, delighting in her softness, the swell of her hips and breasts molded to my palms. My cock is rigid against her thigh. I rock into her, craving the friction we both need. She releases a breathy moan as her nails dig into my back, spurring me on as I thrust against her. We're both still clothed but I can feel the damp heat at the apex of her thighs through the thin barrier of her shorts.

The realization makes me groan. "I need to feel you, all of you." My voice is rough with longing.

Her eyes flutter open, pupils blown wide with desire. She nods, licking her lips in a nervous gesture that makes me ache. I've never wanted anything more in this life than I want her, here and now.

"Please." The single word is my undoing.

I lift her easily into my arms and carry her to the bedroom, kicking the door closed behind us. By the time I lay her on the bed, we're both trembling with need.

CHAPTER 10

LATALIA

Blaine deposits me on the bed, his ability to lift me a massive turn-on. He slowly kisses his way from my neck to my chest then back up to my mouth. His lips are soft and warm against mine. The desire to taste him is overwhelming.

He runs his tongue over my lips and then into my mouth, and I moan. My body reacts to his touch, ready to surrender to him completely. Blaine pulls back biting his bottom lip and studies me still clothed. I move to undress, but he stops me, then steps back to peel off his own clothes. I lay there studying him.

Blaine's body is a work of art, sculpted to perfection from years of working out. His thick cock stands erect, the tip glistening with pre-cum. A silver barbell pierces the underside of his shaft, catching the light with each twitch of his arousal.

I lick my lips, aching to taste him, run my tongue along the ridge of that piercing.

He smirks down at me, knowing exactly what I'm thinking.

"Like what you see?" His voice is a low rumble, stroking over my senses.

"Very much so." I reach for him, dragging my nails down his abdomen. "Now, are you going to join me, or do I need to take matters into my own hands?"

"Patience." Blaine captures my wrists, pinning them above my head. "We're going to go slow. I plan on tasting every inch of you and making you cum so hard you forget your own name."

A delicious shiver runs through me at his words. "Promises, promises."

He silences me with a searing kiss, tongue thrusting into my mouth to tangle with mine. I moan, arching into him, craving the feel of his body against mine.

My heart pounds in my chest, desire and need warring within me. I want this, want him, but the scars marring his torso stand out obstructing my lust. Who hurt him? And will I only add to those wounds?

Blaine pulls back, staring down at me with eyes dark with lust. "Stop thinking so much. I'm here, and I want this. I want you." He emphasizes each word with a roll of his hips, his cock sliding against my clit through my clothes.

Pleasure spikes, breaking through my doubts. I wrap my legs around his waist, grinding against him. "Then take me."

A low growl rumbles in his chest as he claims my mouth again in a bruising kiss. My fingers run up his fade then tangles in his hair, holding him to me as I drown in the taste of him.

Blaine's hands slide under my tank top, smooth fingers skimming up my sides. I shiver as he cups my breasts, squeezing gently. He rolls my nipples between his thumbs and forefingers, the slight pinch sending bolts of pleasure straight to my clit.

I whimper into his mouth. He swallows the sounds greedily, his kisses becoming more demanding.

My pussy throbs, slick and needy. I rock my hips, trying to gain friction where I need it most. Blaine chuckles, the sound vibrating against my lips. He gives my nipples one last pinch before sliding his hands down to grip the hem of my top.

In one smooth motion, he pulls it up and off, baring my breasts to his heated gaze. I stare up at him, for once not fighting to hide my soft curves and stretch marks.

Blaine's eyes gleam with hunger and something more, something that looks suspiciously like reverence. "Gorgeous," he breathes. He slides down my body, planting open-mouthed kisses over my breasts and belly.

My insecurities fade under the devotion in his touch and voice. I relax in the mattress, content to let him worship me.

He dips his tongue into my belly button, then trails lower. His breath ghosts over my pussy, hot even through my shorts, I had opted out of panties this morning to avoid the lines that were printing out through my shorts, and if the feeling I'm having now was the verdict it was a heavenly decision. I squirm, desperate for more but afraid to ask.

Blaine grins up at me, a wicked curve of his lips. "So impatient." He nuzzles between my legs, rubbing his nose over my covered clit.

Pleasure explodes through me. "Blaine!"

"I've got you, kitten." His voice is a low rumble. "Just feel."

He grips the waist of my shorts with his teeth and pulls. The material slides down my legs, baring me to him completely.

My cheeks heat even as my pussy floods with need. Blaine doesn't miss a beat, nuzzling against my bare folds, his nose nudging my clit.

I cry out, back arching off the bed as ecstasy consumes me.

Blaine spreads my legs wider, holding me open for his exploration. His tongue flicks out, teasing my entrance before gliding up to circle my clit.

"Oh God!" I fist the sheets, writhing under the intimate caress.

He sucks my clit into his mouth, flicking it with his tongue. Two fingers slide into my pussy, crooking to find my g-spot.

Pressure builds inside me, heat and pleasure swirling into an inferno. Blaine keeps up his ministrations, relentless as I shatter around him.

My orgasm bursts through me, a supernova behind my eyes. Blaine groans against my pussy, lapping up my release. He kisses his way back up my body, pausing to nip at my breasts. I can taste myself on his lips when he claims my mouth.

Our tongues tangle together, mimicking the act I crave most. My hands roam over his body, memorizing every plane and hollow. I wrap my fingers around his swollen cock. Blaine hisses into the kiss, thrusting into my grip. I stroke him, relearning what gives him pleasure.

"Fuck, baby." He pants against my mouth, eyes squeezed shut. "You keep doing that and this will be over before it starts."

I slow my movements. "I want you to cum for me."

Blaine shakes his head. "Not in your hand but trust me I will."

My pussy clenches at the promise in his voice.

I moan, clutching at his back. The ridge of another scar is rough under my fingers, and I wonder what he must have endured.

Blaine dips his head, taking one of my nipples between his teeth. He sucks hard enough to hurt, the sharp sting melting into pleasure. I cry out, inner walls clamping together.

I run my hands down to grip his pulsing cock, determined to get my tongue on his piercing.

"Sit," I order, biting the inside of my bottom lip.

Blaine meets my gaze. "Yes ma'am"

I release his cock and he sits. I move to position myself between his legs. Taking his cock between my lips, I savor the taste of him. His skin is salty and musky, an aphrodisiac on my tongue. I swirl my tongue around his tip gliding down the length of his shaft, his piercing tickling my tongue. My heart races as I lick and suck, teasing him.

Blaine groans, fists clenching in the sheets. I increase the suction and speed, eager to bring him pleasure. His hips thrust against me involuntarily as I draw circles around his head with my tongue.

He tastes so good, like sex and sin rolled into one. I can feel the tension radiating off Blaine's body as he teeters on the edge of orgasm. I wrap a hand around the base of his cock, working it in tandem with my mouth and tongue. My free hand snakes up to pinch at his nipples, eliciting a deep growl from Blaine's throat that sends shivers through me. My pussy tightens in response to his arousal, dripping onto the bedspread beneath us.

"Fuck Latalia," Blaine gasps out as he buries both hands in my hair, guiding me off his cock. "I want her pussy clenching around me when I cum. But I want to make sure you scatter for me first."

Blaine stands and walks to a chest I hadn't noticed on the opposite side of the room. He returns with the Durex Play ring and a condom in hand, a devilish smirk on his face. My pussy clenches in anticipation, already slick and aching for his touch.

"You ready for this, kitten?" he asks, voice rough with need.

I nod eagerly, spreading my legs in invitation. Blaine kneels between my thighs, leaning down to capture a nipple between his teeth. He suckles and nibbles, sending jolts of pleasure straight to my clit.

With his free hand, Blaine presses the ring onto my clit and presses the button. A low throb begins, intensifying until my hips buck off the bed. Blaine releases my nipple to watch my reaction, eyes dark with lust.

The pulses come in waves, pushing me higher and higher. I'm barely aware of Blaine teasing my nipples and inner thighs, too lost in the sensations overwhelming my clit.

"That's it, baby," Blaine rasps. "Feel it. Let go."

His words break the last of my restraint. I shatter with a scream, vision whiting out as pleasure consumes me. The orgasm seems endless, rolling through my body in crashing tides.

When I come back to myself, Blaine has removed the ring and

is holding me close, murmuring words of praise and love. I cling to him, still trembling in the aftermath.

"You're so fucking gorgeous when you cum," Blaine says reverently. "I could watch you fall apart all day."

A blush steals over my cheeks at his praise. I tilt my head up, meeting his gaze. "Take me again. I want to feel you inside me."

Blaine's eyes darken, pupils blowing wide. "Your wish is my command, baby."

He kisses me deeply as he settles between my thighs once more. I moan into Blaine's mouth, ready to soar again.

Blaine slips on the condom then lines himself up at my opening. He sinks into my slick heat with a groan. I arch into him, relishing the delicious stretch and fullness of his cock. He fills me so perfectly, reaching depths no one else ever has.

"Fuck, you feel amazing," Blaine grits out. He pulls back slowly until just the tip remains inside, then slides home again.

I zero in on the sensation, inner walls fluttering around his length. Blaine sets up a torturous rhythm, withdrawing almost completely before surging forward. He has me writhing beneath him, desperate for more but unable to form the words.

"Tell me what you want, baby," Blaine commands softly. He punctuates his words with a sharp snap of his hips. "I need to hear you say it."

"Harder," I gasp. "Faster. Please, Blaine."

A smug smile curves Blaine's lips. "Your wish is my command."

He picks up the pace, pounding into me with enough force to scoot me up the bed. I wrap my legs around his waist, pulling him in deeper. Blaine braces his hands on either side of my head, gaze locked with mine as he claims my body.

The new angle has him hitting my g-spot with every stroke. Pressure builds at the base of my spine, coiling tighter and tighter. I'm already close to the edge, the orgasm Blaine wrung from me with the vibrator sensitizing my nerves.

"Come for me again," Blaine growls. "I want to feel you come on my cock."

His words send me tumbling over the brink with a cry. My inner walls clamp down on his length as pleasure washes through me. Blaine curses, hips stuttering as he follows me into release.

We cling to each other, waiting for our breathing to slow. Blaine brushes a tender kiss over my brow, eyes soft with affection. "You're incredible, you know that?"

A blush steals over my cheeks. I duck my head, overwhelmed by the emotion in his voice and gaze. "So are you."

Blaine smiles, the expression lighting up his face. "We're pretty incredible together."

My heart swells at his words. Together. I could get used to the sound of that.

Blaine eases out of me with a groan and ties off the condom, disposing of it in the trash bin beside the bed. I roll onto my side, watching through half-lidded eyes as he cleans up in the ensuite bathroom. By the time he emerges, I've drifted into a light doze.

The mattress dips as Blaine climbs back into bed, molding his body along my back and wrapping an arm around my waist. His breath tickles the nape of my neck, lips brushing over the sensitive skin.

I blow out a breath. "I could lie here all day, but I gave Trixton my word that you'd get to all your shoots today, and on time."

Blaine laughs. "Do you ever just turn your work brain off?"

"I do," I admit turning in his arms to face him. "I did. Thank you for that, by the way. It was an amazing escape from my brain." I plant a quick kiss on his lips. "But now, its time to turn it back on. So, enough lipping. Let's go get ready."

Blaine smiles but he doesn't protest.

CHAPTER 11

I stand by the entrance of the cavernous studio, all polished concrete floors and high ceilings, taking a moment to inhale the scent of newness. Everything here is sleek and modern, meant to evoke a cool sensuality. The perfect setting for an underwear shoot.

My gaze sweeps over the organized chaos of the set, crew members efficiently setting up lights and cameras, models in various states of undress as they get prepped by makeup artists and hair stylists.

In the center of it all is Blaine, casually chatting with the photographer as he slips on a pair of snug black boxer briefs. They hug his muscular thighs and emphasize the generous bulge at his groin, making my mouth go dry. I force myself to look away, heat flooding my cheeks. *This is a professional outing.* I sternly remind myself. I need to focus on the task at hand, gathering feedback on Blaine and his public image to create a better media campaign.

"Latalia, over here!" Blaine waves me over with an easy smile, seemingly unbothered by his state of undress. Of course, he's used to it, stripping down is part of his job.

I move to join him, offering a polite smile to the photographer in greeting. "I didn't expect it to be so..." I gesture around at the chaos. "Involved."

Blaine chuckles, the sound rumbling in his broad chest. "Photoshoots are rarely as glamorous as the final product suggests. But Theo here is a genius, he'll make it worth the effort."

"Flatterer," the photographer scoffs without heat, attention already back on his camera.

"Just honest," Blaine says, eyes gleaming with mirth as they meet mine.

I smile over to Theo, stretching my hand. "Latalia Brown." Theo accepts returning my smile. "I'm working on a campaign for Mr. Dixon's public image and was wondering if you could spare five minutes to answer a few questions?"

Theo nods, and Blaine smiles.

"I'll head to make-up," Blaine says, resting a hand on my shoulder that sends heat flooding through me.

I clear my throat as I nod.

"Thank you for doing this," I begin once Blaine is out of earshot. "I won't take up too much of your time, I just have about two questions. Before I dive in, do you consent with me taking a quote from your answer for the social media aspect of the campaign?"

"Of course," Theo responds. "Blaine gets a bad rep. He's honestly one of the easiest models I work with on his good days."

That gives me pause. "His good days?"

Theo nods. "When he's on top of his game, he's gold. I know I'll get my shot in one or two takes. But some days are ... difficult." Theo shrugs. "But that could be said for about anyone, right? I mean we all have bad days."

I glance over to Blaine. He sits in a folding chair at the side of the set with two women getting him ready, one touching up his make-up and the other teasing the short nappy curls on the top of his head. It's hard not to wonder about what he must go through behind the walls he erects around his life.

The old wounds covering his torso return to my mind. They aren't there now, which tells me they must put him through body make-up too before he comes on set. His gaze catches mine and I offer a warm smile.

"Of course," I say, returning my attention to Theo. "So, would you say, you look forward to seeing his name on your call list then when you have difficult shoots planned?"

"I guess you could say that," Theo says, nodding in thought. "Blaine would be on my list of select few."

"That's great to hear." I smile. "Final question, what would you say to the rumors escalating that Mr. Dixon is often problematic on set?"

"Those claims are wild, to say the least," Theo says. "I've worked with problematic model diva types before and believe me, Blaine isn't it."

"Perfect," I say with a curt nod. "That's all the questions I had. Thanks so much for your time."

Theo turns to go position his camera by the first set and Blaine comes up behind me using his fingers to tickle the dip in my back along my spinal cord.

"Shouldn't you be getting ready instead of distracting me?" I arch a brow, willing my voice to remain steady.

"What's the rush?" Blaine shrugs, leaning in close enough for me to catch his cologne. "The star of the show can be fashionably late."

My eyes narrow, noticing the smug tilt of his lips. "Is that so, Mr. Dixon,' I tease, reaching back in my pocket for my notepad and pen. "Is that a direct quote for my campaign? I'm sure it would do wonders for your image."

"You really never take off that professional hat, do you?"

Blaine concedes with an exaggerated roll of his eyes. "I guess duty calls."

He winks at me before sauntering over to get in front of the cameras, the playful roll of his hips making it clear he's putting on a show.

I shake my head at his antics, a surge of fondness mingling with my exasperation. Blaine has always enjoyed riling me up, his playful nature both endearing and frustrating.

My attention is drawn to the set as the photographer starts giving directions, multiple assistants rushing to arrange props and lighting. A makeup artist dabs at Blaine's face, expertly accentuating his striking features, though they opt not to cover up the thin scar under his eye.

I know he still struggles with insecurities stemming from a turbulent childhood, but I wasn't sure how that played into all of this yet.

Shaking off the unpleasant thought, I focus on the present. Blaine eases into the first pose with a graceful power that steals my breath, muscles flexing and shifting under smooth, milk chocolate skin.

The trunks he's wearing leave little to the imagination, clinging obscenely to his hips and doing nothing to hide the sizable bulge between his thighs. Heat floods my cheeks as I stare, transfixed by the sight. I can almost imagine how he would feel, hard and thick under my curious hands, silky soft skin covering rigid flesh.

A flare of possessiveness rises in my chest at the thought of other women seeing him like this, desiring what I wished belonged to me. But that's ridiculous, I chide myself. Blaine isn't mine to claim, we haven't even been on a real date yet. I'm here as his publicist, to do a job, not to ogle his magnificent body.

Summoning my willpower, I force my gaze away from Blaine. The other models on set, however, provide little distraction from the jealous thoughts playing out in my mind. Lush curves barely concealed by scraps of lace and silk, sun-kissed skin and coy smiles all with eyes trained on Blaine. I sigh. This is turning out to be a long day.

Swallowing hard, I pull out my phone and open the Sisterhood chat with Natasha, Kamilla, and Trina. Maybe talking with my girls will provide a welcome distraction from the temptation surrounding me.

Me:

So, funny story. Remember the photoshoot I told you about for Blaine?

Trina:

Of course! How's it going? Did you get some good quotes for his publicity campaign?

Me:

That part is going perfectly. But everything else... is going downhill fast. I may have underestimated how difficult it would be to stay professional with Blaine parading around in next to nothing.

Natasha:

Girl, you did not! Are you telling us this photoshoot is getting steamy? I need details, stat!

A FLUSH CRAWLS up my neck as I think about how to respond. My friends know I'm attracted to Blaine, but I'm starting to have a bit more of an emotional pull to him as well that I'm not sure if I'm ready to admit to as yet.

Me:

You have no idea. They've got him in these tiny swim trunks, and he looks...incredible. All I can think about is peeling them off of him! I know I'm here for work, but how am I supposed to focus with that temptation in front of me? Plus, there are so many gorgeous women here also half naked that are all up on him.

KAMILLA:

Is that a bit of jealousy, I'm detecting? I think our girl is starting to catch feelings for Mr. Hotness over there. On a more serious note, Girl, you're only human! No one could blame you for being distracted by a fine man in little clothes. Plus, if that man wants you none of those skinny little Heffers can take his eye away from you.

TRINA:

Kam is right, Tals. You work so hard. You should enjoy yourself when the opportunity arises. And if Blaine is respecting your presence by not entertaining the other women around then it sounds like the perfect opportunity just fell into your lap!

THEIR ENCOURAGEMENT HELPS EASE my anxiety over the conflicting feelings I feel for Blaine. My girls are right, I always sabotage myself with work whenever there's something, or in this case someone, not work related that I want. It's alright to give in to temptation every now and then. And the temptation of Blaine's body is one I find irresistible. I opt not to dive into details about the second steamy encounter I had with Blaine earlier, instead I snap a quick photo of Blaine and send it to the group chat with the caption, "What do you call being stuck on set with this magnificent view?"

My phone blows up immediately with their enthusiastic responses.

NATASHA:

Hot damn, that view makes me know there is a God! Girl, you hit the jackpot.

TRINA:

I may need a cold shower after seeing that! No wonder you're distracted, I would be too if I were around all that!

KAMILLA:

The only appropriate response to that view is: Hallelujah! You better climb that like a tree, sis, before someone else does!

THEIR EXCITEMENT and praise of Blaine's physique only makes the heat swirling inside me intensify. I bow out of the chat, telling them I needed to get back to work and leaving their imaginations to run wild.

Smiling, I watch Blaine pose with an effortless poise in front of the camera, muscles flexing and glistening under the bright lights. Theo encourages him to 'look brooding and mysterious', but I much prefer his radiant smile. If only I could be the one behind the lens, capturing intimate moments between us.

I clear my throat and fan myself, hoping to abate the flush creeping over my skin. At this rate, I'll be a puddle on the floor before the photoshoot finishes. The idea of 'climbing him like a tree' as Kamilla suggested is becoming increasingly appealing. But I have to stay professional - this is still my job, and I can't let my personal feelings interfere. Even if the 'star of this show' is testing my self-control in the most delicious way possible.

I retreat to the ladies' room, barreling into a stall to escape the sight of Blaine before I do something I regret. The cool air of the hallway helps clear my mind, and I take a few deep breaths to steady my racing pulse. This fierce attraction to Blaine threatens to override my better judgment, but I can't lose control. I've worked too hard to jeopardize everything for a fleeting moment of passion.

Two models come in after me, casually discussing their lustful intentions towards Blaine in explicit terms. Their words are blatant and certainly not professional. Desperate to get eyes on the women who were clearly oblivious to my presence, I prop open the stall door just enough to catch a glimpse of them.

"Did you see the way he was looking at us?" The blonde model smirks, running a hand through her hair. "He was undressing us with his eyes, probably imagining all the dirty things he wants to do to us."

"Mmm, I bet he's into some kinky stuff," her friend purrs. "Maybe a little bondage, some spanking. I wouldn't mind if he wanted to tie me up."

The blonde sighs. "Too bad he's one of those reclusive types, he's so caught up in the shoot that you have to work twice as hard to get him to even take you out for coffee."

The friend scoffs. "Girl please, I can get around Blaine Dixon easy. Have you seen the press behind him lately?" She leans into the mirror to touch up her mascara. "All we'd have to do is threatened to tell the press he was inappropriate with us on set, and he'd play ball."

They laugh and my hands clench into fists, rage simmering beneath my skin. It takes immense effort to remain still and not confront them for their disrespect. Blaine is not some plaything for their twisted fantasies. And he's already working so damn hard to clear his name in the press.

"God, I just want to rip off those swim trunks and ride him all night long," the blonde continues with a throaty moan. "Bet he'd love to be ridden hard."

Her friend laughs, the sound grating. "Whether he wants to or not. I'm gonna get what I want from that fine piece of ass."

Revulsion rises in my throat like bile at their words. My nails dig into my palms, the pain barely registering through my anger. How dare they? If they think they are going to bribe Blaine with some convoluted story in the press they have a next guess coming.

I step forward, rage etched into every line of my face as I prepare to confront them for their audacity. No one disrespects Blaine like this, not on my watch. They have no idea who they're dealing with, but they're about to find out.

"Tip to the wise, or unwise in your case, maybe you should ensure the room is empty before you share your convoluted plans." My voice emerges as a sinister hiss.

The models startle, expressions morphing into confusion at my sudden appearance.

"This is a private conversation," the brunette says with a frown, her eyes narrowing in suspicion.

I arch a brow, anger simmering in my gaze. "Private? I could hear your delusional plans from the Eiffel freaking Tower. Did you really think you could get away with fucking with Blaine that way?"

The blonde scoffs, though unease flickers in her eyes. She's intelligent enough to recognize I may not be someone to trifle with. "We were just joking around. Mind your own business."

I laugh to myself that come out more bitter than I'd intended. "You made it my business the moment you decided to threaten Blaine Dixon's career and public image." I pull my phone from my purse and ask Google to dial Victor Suarez, the CEO of the largest modeling agency and trending castor director in the industry.

"Hi Vick," I say, placing the phone on speaker and locking my gaze on the chatty brunette.

"Tali Darling," Victor responds. "It's been far too long."

"It has hasn't it," I respond, my tone laced with fake enthusiasm. "I'm so sorry to bother you, I know how busy you are with the international editorial campaigns, and the new movie deal. Congrats on that by the way."

The blonde model shifts uncomfortably as her mouth dips open just a tad.

"Just another day at the office," Victor responds.

"You work far too hard," I say, with forced laughter. "Anyway, I just wanted to let you know that I have relaunched my agency and will be sure to shoot any recommendations I come across for models or actors on my side of the pond that may be a good fit for endorsement or representation." I shift my gaze back to the brunette. "And, of course, those to avoid."

"You have always been so good to me Tali," Victor says. "We must catch up soon."

"I'll be sure to make that happen when next I'm in Cali. Talk soon."

I hang up, and take a predatory step forward, relishing the fresh flicker of fear and understanding in their eyes. They have no idea of the lengths I'll go to in order to protect the people I care for. "Let me make myself perfectly clear—if either of you so much as look at Blaine the wrong way, I'll make sure your careers in this industry are over before you can blink. Do you understand me?"

The models glance at each other, swallowing in unison. When they face me again, their arrogance has vanished, replaced by wariness.

"Who are you?" the brunette asks, her voice trembling.

I smirk. "My name is irrelevant as I doubt either of you will ever get the privilege of working with me." Threats are unnecessary now that they understand the level of influence I wield.

"Stay away from Blaine," I say with finality.

With murmurs of agreement, they scurry from the restroom like rats fleeing from a sinking ship. I wait until the door swings shut behind them before releasing a slow breath, the anger seeping from my body.

My heels click against the tiled floor as I emerge from the restroom, scanning the bustling set for Blaine. He's surrounded by crew members, deep in discussion about the next shot. Even from across the room, I can see the tension lining his broad shoulders, detect the strain in his smile. The scowl marring his handsome features whenever one of the female models sidles up to him only confirms my suspicions—their blatant advances grates on his nerves too.

Blaine glances up, black eyes meeting mine from beneath the thick fan of his lashes. A myriad of emotions flit through their stormy depths before his lips curve into a slow, breathtaking smile. My heart stutters at the sight, heat flooding my cheeks when I recall the conversation I interrupted in the restroom. For all their vile intentions, those women weren't entirely mistaken in their assessment of Blaine's charisma. He wields it like a weapon without realizing the damage it inflicts on my composure.

Shaking off the flustered sensation, I weave through the organized chaos towards Blaine. He breaks away from the group with an apology, meeting me halfway.

"Everything okay?" Worry creases his brow as he searches my face. "You look upset."

"Just taking care of a small problem." I shrug, hoping to brush off his concern. The last thing I need is for him to discover I threatened anyone on his behalf. "The shoot's going well I see."

"As always, a circus," he says dryly, raking a hand through his hair. "But we're making progress."

"Good. Keep at it." I nod in the direction of the set. "I should head out, lots of work waiting for me back at the house. I'll meet up with you later. " I turn to leave then remembered who I'm dealing with. "Try to stay out of trouble today, would you? For me?"

Blaine smiles and flashes me a devilish wink. I shake my head then turn to leave. His gaze follows me as I make my way off the set, a steady warmth against my back.

CHAPTER 12

BLAINE

"That's it for today everyone," Theo announces. "We think we got it."

I breathe a sigh of relief for the first time in a while. It was a smooth day. Of course, it does help that it started with Latalia in my bed. A smile caresses my lips at the thought. But it was more than just that. The usually handsy models I worked with today actually kept their hands to themselves, and we wrapped on time.

My muscles ache pleasantly from the physically demanding poses, a familiar burn I'm learning to enjoy. As the crew begins packing up the set, I shoot a message to Latalia to let her know that I'm done for the day and ask her to meet me in the lobby dressed to be catered to. There are no added details in my message, but she doesn't protest.

Eager to wash the layers of makeup from my body, I head to my dressing room, grateful that Trixton always ensured my sets had a small shower.

The hot water cascades over my head and down my back,

soothing my tired muscles. I close my eyes, replaying the day's shoot in my mind. Despite the relative ease of the shoot, my thoughts kept drifting to Latalia. The curve of her lips. The spark in her eyes. The warmth of her touch.

A smile tugs at the corner of my lips as a memory of the first evening she moved in fills my mind. I remember how flustered she was the night she came to tell me she'd be using the pool. I had hoped to tease her by lounging in just my boxers, and her barely-there bikini drove me wild. The memory makes my cock pulse.

My eyes fly open as I realize I've been standing under the spray, lost in thought, far longer than necessary. With a chuckle, I turn off the water and reach for a towel. Latalia's unintentional seduction seems to have left its mark on me in more ways than one.

Excited to spend more time with the woman that has captured my mind, I get dressed and head out to meet Latalia. Today's photoshoot may have gone smoothly, but I have a feeling the evening will be far more demanding. And I plan to rise to the challenge.

When I meet up with Latalia, she is dressed to kill in a figure-hugging pair of faded jeans that accentuate her ass, and a single shoulder striped top. She looks up as I approach, a slow smile curving her lips.

"How was the shoot?" she asks, her husky voice like a caress.

"Uneventful," I say, leaning in to brush a kiss across her cheek in greeting. I inhale the scent of her, warm and spicy, and have to stifle a groan. "But you were on my mind the whole time."

A blush stains her cheeks, her eyes sparkling with amusement and desire. "Is that so?"

"You know it is." I offer her my arm. "Shall we?"

She takes it, her soft body pressed against mine as we head out to the car. "So, I'm dressed and here as agreed with two whole hours to spare before your session with Dr. Reid. Now can you tell me what the big surprise is?" She asks.

"Fine. I'm taking you for an early dinner at that new Italian place you mentioned you've been wanting to try. Then..." I pause, meeting her gaze. "Dessert at home after my session if you're up to it."

I see the flare of heat in her eyes and grin. Our 'desserts' are always memorable.

The drive to the restaurant is filled with light, teasing conversation and the occasional caress - her hand on my thigh, her fingers grazing the back of my neck. By the time we arrive, the simmering desire has built to a slow burn, every touch and glance stoking the flames.

I guide Latalia into the warmly lit dining room of the new Italian place. The soft strains of a violin drift over from the corner, the notes pirouetting in the air. I pull out her chair, and she slides in, a coy smile lighting her face.

"The place is nice, don't you think?" she asks, her eyes drinking in the rustic interior, the way the lights play off the wooden paneling.

"I think the company is even better," I quip, causing her to blush. I take my seat, and our waiter comes over, menus in hand.

We stare at the menus, our heads close as we scroll through the array of pasta dishes that pop up. "Penne Arrabbiata," I say, pointing at the picture of the vibrant red dish garnished with a sprig of basil.

She lifts an eyebrow, the corner of her mouth twisting in a playful smirk. "Are you sure, Blaine? That's a little...spicy. Think you can handle the heat?"

I laugh, a low rumble that gets her to look up at me with twinkling eyes. "Heat?" I feign horror. "I must've forgotten to mention that I was forged in the fires of spicy food."

"Oh, a culinary phoenix, are we?" She grins, her eyes brimming with mirth.

"Something like that," I say, holding her gaze. A small chuckle escapes her, a soft sound that sends warmth coursing through me.

"I am leaning more towards Fettuccine Alfredo," she muses, her fingers tracing the name on the menu. "It's rich, creamy, comforting. It's...tame compared to the Arrabbiata." She meets my eyes. "But just as satisfying."

"Are you sure you don't want a shot at taming the 'culinary phoenix'," I shoot back, watching her break into a fit of laughter.

"Maybe," she says, her voice dropping to a conspiratorial whisper as she regains her composure.

We settle on the 'Taste of Italy' platter, a mixed array of the restaurant's best dishes. As the waiter is about to retreat with our order, Latalia stops him, her eyes sparkling with a secret.

"Add a bottle of Chianti to that," she says, looking at me with a devilish grin. "We need something to tame a phoenix after all."

The waiter nods, hiding a smile before he leaves us. I shake my head at her, but inside, I'm stoked. There's something about the spark in her eyes that sends a thrill through me.

She's challenging me, teasing me, pulling on a side of me that I'd kept hidden for years.

When the food arrives, it's a symphony of smells and colors. Hearty meatballs nestled in marinara sauce, ribbons of pasta swirled in creamy sauces, and a smattering of colorful veggies complete the ensemble.

Latalia offers me the first bite, her fingers deftly wrapping a forkful of fettuccine. I lean forward, my lips closing around the fork. The taste of the rich, creamy sauce dances on my tongue, the flavors bursting with authenticity.

"Good?" she asks, her lips quirked in a hopeful smile.

"Incredible," I confirm, watching her face light up.

Her smile widens. "Perfect, now that I see the food didn't take you out, I can enjoy my meal."

My eyes grow wide, as I chuckle. "Oh, your plan was to take me out, huh."

"Not at all," she responds, "But one of us had to take the fall for the team and I figured it should be the least pretty one out of the two."

We both laugh.

I lift my glass to her. "Touché."

Our gazes lock over the rim of our wine glasses, and the electricity in the air is almost palpable. She playfully swipes a bit of sauce from my lip with her thumb, and my heart lurches at the intimate gesture. Her touch lingers, and I press a soft kiss to her thumb, her eyes widening in surprise before a slow smile stretches across her face.

Between bites and sips of wine, Latalia turns to me, her eyes softening with concern. "Blaine, how's your mom doing?" she asks, the playful undertone of our dinner conversation abruptly taking a more serious turn. Latalia's question about my mother comes like a soft breeze, a sincere care in her voice. My heart aches a little at the mention of my mother, the image of her gaunt face, lost eyes flashing through my mind. I clutch my wine glass a bit tighter, the coolness grounding me.

"She's... She's getting better," I begin, the words coming out more confident than I feel. "I've finally started taking the steps to get her into a long-term live-in facility." The edge of my lips lift slightly, a mirthless smile. "It's more equipped than the small hospice she's been in. It can... provide her with the help she needs."

Latalia's fingers gently trace the back of my hand, a soft touch of understanding and support that makes something clench inside me. Her silence speaks volumes, and her nod is the only acknowledgment I need to know she's there for me.

"How about you," I ask. "What is your family dynamic like."

Latalia shrugs. "I have a younger sister, though most people think we're twins. She's five years younger than I am, but she swears she's my mom."

We share a laugh.

"And your parents?" I ask, hoping to learn even more about her world.

Latalia goes silent, and I know I've struck a nerve. Our gazes lock, and in that moment, I see the delicate fabric of courage weaving through her.

Taking a deep breath, she begins to speak, her voice quivering. "My parent are dead, well at least they are to me." Her fingers clutch her wine glass, knuckles whitening. "My sister Trina and I... we didn't have an easy childhood." She takes a shaky breath, her voice carrying a trace of vulnerability I've never heard from her before. "I was around five when my dad started...changing. Mom had just given birth to Trina and he..." her voice breaks, but she takes another deep breath and continues. "The booze took hold of him. It made him a monster." Her fingers absent-mindedly trace the rim of her wine glass, her gaze distant as if she's reliving the past.

I take her hand from the glass in mine and give her a reassuring squeeze.

"We were his punching bags," she continues. "Me more so than Trina, probably because she was just a baby. He'd come home in the middle of the night, reeking of alcohol and full of rage. I remember hiding under the bed, praying he wouldn't find me."

Her words paint a cruel image, one filled with shadows and screams, of a home turned into a battlefield. My free hand balls into a fist, clenching on the tablecloth, rage simmering in my veins at the thought of a man harming his own children.

"But he always did," she whispers, her voice brittle. Her eyes meet mine, holding an ocean of unsaid pain. "I was his favorite punching bag. But you know what? I'm stronger for it. I'm here. He didn't break me."

A surge of white-hot anger courses through me, ferocious and raw, at the thought of her tormented past. The image of that small, terrified girl hiding under her bed makes my blood boil. A growl, guttural and primal, rumbles in my chest. I want to tear apart the man who hurt her, who transformed her childhood into a living nightmare. For a moment, I'm rendered mute, fighting to tame the storm of anger before I can trust myself to speak.

Latalia's courage though is stunning, her resilience, awe-inspiring.

She chuckles, the sound hollow. "I've seen monsters, Blaine. I've faced them and survived. And that has made all the difference. It's made me...me. So, I found my own family. I've my sister Trina, and my two best friends, Kamilla and Natasha."

"I'm sorry, Latalia," I manage to choke out, my voice thick with anger. "I'm so, so sorry."

She smiles, but her eyes are sad. "Don't be. It's taught me that I can survive anything. Even my own past." She sighs. "I'm not perfect and I wish I could say I had it all together. But I don't. I've always felt like I was too tall, or my hips were too wide," she explains. "Like I was never enough... Like my father used to tell me in his rage or my ex, Jaden constantly reminded me whenever I would ask for something he didn't think I deserved."

She pauses, a stray tear streaming down her face, I stretch my free hand over and brush it away.

"Wait, is that why you thought I wouldn't have wanted you to stick around that first night?" I ask, understanding setting in.

Her gaze falls to the table as she nods. "Because of all the shit I went through with my parents I was too scared to speak up for myself and I let Jaden walk all over me in that relationship. He completely obliterated my self-esteem. And convinced me that an ogre would have better luck at love than I could."

Bile rises in my throat at the thought of Latalia blaming herself for anything either of those shit faced assholes did to her. Or worse believing any of their crap.

I tilt her chin, so I could see her eyes and she forced a smile.

"That asshole ex of yours clearly had no fucking clue what he was talking about. Because you are beautiful inside and out. Not everyone understands how to care for a diamond." I smile. "But I know a rare find when I see one."

The memories of her abusive relationship still haunt her eyes. Yet, amidst all the darkness, there's light when she smiles.

"Thank you. I've been working with my therapist a lot to help me see myself as the gem you guys see," she admits. "It's been a great outlet for me, and I want it to do the same for you. Then maybe if you find that it helps over time you could recommend it to Blair. You know, pay it forward to those you care about."

You're who I'm starting to care about. I want to say. "Thank you," I say instead. "For trusting me enough to share that with me and for believing I can somehow be a better person even with me fighting you every step of the way."

That last bit makes her smile. I bring her hand to my lips and give it a light kiss. This glimpse into her strength, her resilience, only grows my respect for her. And though I still have my concerns about doing this whole therapy thing, I'll give it my best shot. For her.

The cheque arrives, and I pay it before leading her out of the restaurant over to the therapist's office conveniently located across the street.

"You ready for this?" she asks, the twinkle returning to her beautiful brown eyes.

"I guess I have to be," I say swallowing my nerves as we make our way to the inside.

Latalia guides me over to a desk where a receptionist directs us to fill out some paperwork.

"I've been here tons of times," Latalia confesses. "Dr. Reid knows what she's about. You can trust her."

I nod. Once the paperwork is complete, the receptionist tells me I can head over to Dr. Reid's office.

Latalia smiles. "I really think you'll get a lot out of this experience. I'll be right out here if you need anything."

"Thank you." I say, swallowing my nerves.

She squeezes my arm. "You've got this. Just be honest with Dr. Reid. This will help you in the long run, I promise."

Summoning my courage, I knock on the door. A warm voice bids me enter. With Latalia's words echoing in my mind, I step into the room. Dr. Reid rises with a smile, shaking my hand and gesturing for me to sit across from her.

"You must be Blaine," a striking older woman with glossy gray hair greets me as I enter. "I'm Dr. Angela Reid. It's a pleasure to meet you. Please, make yourself comfortable."

I draw in a breath, then return her smile.

"Today, I just want us to get to know each other and discuss your goals for therapy," she explains.

I release a slow breath, reassured by her friendly demeanor. Maybe this won't be so bad after all.

I settle into the armchair across from Dr. Reid, the leather creaking under me. "Thank you for seeing me today. To be honest, I'm a bit nervous about all this."

Dr. Reid meets me with a reassuring smile. "That's perfectly normal. Therapy can be an intimidating process, but my goal is to provide a safe and judgment-free space for you to explore your thoughts and feelings about whatever is on your mind."

Her tone puts me further at ease. "What exactly can I expect from these sessions? What are you expecting from me exactly?"

"We'll proceed at your own pace," Dr. Reid explains. "Through our conversations, we'll work to gain insight into experiences that have shaped you, identify any unhealthy patterns of thinking or behavior, and make a plan to enact positive changes in your life. The more open and honest you are, the more you will benefit. Everything we discuss will remain confidential. I generally like to start with a little bit about your past so I can get to understand the person you are in the present. Is that okay?"

I swallow and give her a pained nod. I grasp the armrests of my chair.

It's now or never - time to bare my soul to this stranger in hopes of magically confronting the shadows lurking within.

"My past? Let's see. My past hasn't been an easy one," I admit. "My father left when I was young and my mother..." I trail off, old memories surfacing like sharks in bloody water. "She had her own issues. Let's just say I learned from an early age that I couldn't depend on anyone but myself. It's made trusting people difficult, to say the least."

"I see," Dr. Reid says gently. "Abandonment at a young age can really affect us if not addressed. It's understandable that you would develop defenses to protect yourself emotionally. However, those same defenses can isolate us and prevent intimate relationships. With work, we can overcome them."

No shit.

"Is that something you'd be willing to us exploring further as our sessions progress," Dr. Reid asks, studying me.

I shrug. "You're the doctor," I say, my tone far more critical than I'd meant. "I just mean we can start, wherever you see fit."

Dr. Reid smiles, pulling out a notepad and pen. "Let's start by going back to the beginning."

CHAPTER 13

LATALIA

The car ride back to the house is strained. Blaine hasn't really said much since exiting Dr. Reid's office other than it went well and he needed time to process, and being no stranger to therapy, I respected that. We step through the doors of his house, the familiar scent of lemon furniture polish greeting me. The cleaners had popped by while I'd been leaving earlier, and they had done a great job.

Blaine remains silent beside me, lost in his own thoughts. His brooding expression and tense shoulders inform me of the demons he's wrestling with. I resist the urge to ask him to elaborate in fear that I'd only make things worse.

Instead, I lead him over to the sitting room couch and he sits. He releases a slow breath and drags his gaze to meet mine. Something flickers in his eyes, a shadow of pain and uncertainty. Then it's gone, hidden behind the mask he's so adept at wearing.

"There's nothing to talk about." His tone is gruff and dismissive. "I'm fine."

Liar. The word lingers on the tip of my tongue, but I swallow it back. Pushing him will only make him retreat further. I have to be patient, give him space until he's ready to open up.

With a soft sigh, I nod and sit next to him. "Okay. I'm here if you want to talk. I mean it. You can talk to me about anything."

A flicker of warmth ignites in his gaze. He lifts his hand, brushing a stray curl behind my ear. "I know." His lips curve into a faint, tender smile, and some of the tension eases from my chest. "You're one of the only people I feel I can truly tell anything."

His words make me smile. Recommending therapy was the right move, I know that from both a professional and personal standpoint. His public image showed him on a spiral. In my heart I know it was for the best. But seeing him like this, closed off, broken makes me a tad worried I may have pushed him before he was truly ready.

I give his arm a gentle squeeze. "I'll be in my office working, okay. Feel free to let me know if you need anything. Anything at all."

With a small nod, we stand, and Blaine disappears down the hall toward the living room. I head into my office and power up my laptop, pulling up the documents for Blaine's social media campaign. Immersed in reviewing the schedule of posts and making adjustments, time slips by quickly.

My phone buzzes on the desk, startling me from my focus. A text from Jaden pops up on the screen.

JADEN:

Do you have time to talk?

I STARE AT THE MESSAGE, hesitating, before tapping out a reply.

Me:
Not now. Busy with work.

Guilt twinges in my gut as I set the phone face down on my desk, pushing thoughts of Jaden from my mind. I shouldn't feel guilty for prioritizing my work and my relationship, or lack thereof, with Blaine. Jaden and I have been over for months. He needs to accept that and move on.

Shaking off the unpleasant sensation, I refocus on the documents in front of me. The faster I finish, the sooner I can check on Blaine. I have to make sure he's doing okay, that he's not retreating into those dark places in his mind. He needs me, and I'm gonna be there whenever he's ready to let me in.

Sometime later, a soft knock sounds at the door. I glance up from my laptop to find Blaine hovering in the doorway, hands stuffed in his pockets and gaze averted.

"Have a minute?" He asks, his voice is hesitant, rough with emotion.

"Of course." I close the laptop to give him my full attention. "Come on in."

He steps into the room but remains near the door, shifting his weight from foot to foot. I want nothing more than to go to him, wrap my arms around his shoulders and reassure him that whatever is bothering him, we'll work through it together. But I know if I make any sudden movements, he's liable to bolt like a frightened deer.

"Therapy was...difficult today." He rakes a hand through his hair, mussing the styled strands. "We talked about some things from my childhood, and it brought up a lot of shit I thought I'd buried years ago."

My heart aches at the pain etched into his handsome features.

I know how hard it is to dig up old wounds and relive past traumas.

"I'm so sorry, baby…Blaine." I swallow, kicking myself for allowing the endearment to slip out.

He offers a weak smile, though it doesn't reach his eyes.

"I think I like baby better," he teases.

I twist my mouth to keep from sighing and he laughs."

"I don't know why I'm having such a hard time with this," Blaine admits. "My life is so good now, better than it's ever been. I have a career I tolerate, financial security, and…I found you."

I smile and start to close the space between one slow step at a time.

He sighs. "But it feels like the past still has this hold on me and I can't shake it."

"If the small bit of information I see in the magazines about you is right, you lived through you've been through some form of shit too," I say gently. "The effects of that don't just disappear because your circumstances have changed. It's a long process to heal from emotional trauma and abuse. But what's important is that you're doing the work, and I'm here for you every step of the way."

His gaze lifts to meet mine, a glint in his eyes. "What exactly did you read in those magazines about me?"

"You know…stuff," I reply without hesitation. I smile. "Enough to know that you're not the monster people think you are."

Blaine smiles, slow and sweet, the first genuine smile I've seen from him since we got home. He pulls me into his arms and holds me close, his cheek resting against the top of my head.

We stand there for a long moment, content in the comfort of each other's embrace.

"You know," he says softly, "we've never really talked about my past or what I went through. I got so caught up in erecting these walls that I never stopped to see you were worth letting in."

He pulls back to look at me, eyes troubled. "My past was

fucked up Latalia. There are thinks I went through that I'm not sure you even want to know."

I cup his face in my hands, my heart opening for this complicated, caring man. "I didn't push before because I assumed you had a lot to work through, and you can't pour from an empty cup. I'm happy to support you whenever and however you feel comfortable. You may not know me that well yet, but that's just who I am."

"But I want to." His hands cover mine, holding them in place. "Get to know you better, I mean. To be there for you in more than just your bed. You've been there for me more in the past few days alone than people I've known my whole life. That helps me see glimpses into who you are...the real you. And I think I'm finally ready to allow you to see the real me too."

His words undo me. I've always been the strong one to everyone around me, the shoulder to cry on, even when I was at my most broken stages inside. The idea of Blaine being there to comfort me the way I have for him threatens to crack me wide open in the most glorious, terrifying way.

"I'd like that," I manage to get out, and he pulls me close before leading me over to my bed for us to sit."

"You opened up to me about your childhood earlier, and it may come as a surprise as I'm such a 'well-adjusted' human being," Blaine begins, sarcasm lacing his tone. "But I didn't have an easy childhood either."

I twist on the bed to face him as he continues.

"As you saw, my mom is an addict. She's had a drug problem for years. It started when my dad left. Blair and I, we were six years old the first time she came back home high. And I don't really remember all of it clearly, but I remember lying to our neighbor the next day that we had gone to school and gotten home early after being home alone all day because our mom had forgotten us. Things got a little better after that for about a year or so until they just weren't. Mom had still been using during that time, but she'd always been home. The next year however she started hanging out with Danny, who I found out later was the local pimp on the block." Blaine pauses to suck in a steadying breath.

"Danny made everything worse. Suddenly there were needles everywhere and random men that would come in and out. On Christmas night that year after Danny had left mom shot up with her needles and told me that she'd be up in a bit to tuck us in." Blaine swallows and drops his gaze to the ground. "That night, at seven years old, I got my first blow job from my mother. And what's even more fucked up about that was that I liked it. I didn't know at the time how fucked up it was for my own mother to be 'loving' me that way. I thought it was normal." Blaine's hand balls into a fist as he grips the sheet and I rest my hand on top of his.

"There was no way you could've known at that age that it was wrong," I say, trying to reassure him. "You can't blame yourself for that."

"I thought it was fucking normal, Talia," he exclaims. "I allowed her to do it every holiday for three fucking years until I bragged about the tradition my mother and I was going to do over fourth of July weekend to someone I thought was my friend at school and got made fun off for it. That weekend when I told her no, she tried to go for Blair, and I blocked the door. We had adjoining rooms. She started beating me with my table lamp screaming for me to get out the fucking way." He swallows. "It broke on my forehead and sliced me below my eye. Blair heard the commotion and called 911. That was the first time we were put into social services."

"Oh Blaine." I pull him closer.

"Of course, I didn't tell the authorities the full story in fear it would only make things worse. I told them my mom and her friends had a party and took drugs and that while trying to tuck me in she knocked over the lamp on my head. Looking back now, I doubt anyone believed me. But they allowed my mom to take us back after being clean for a year and going to rehab. But of course, the bliss didn't last."

He sighs. "I could go on and on about trauma, you know. I could complain about being the one who has to turn around and financially take care of the woman who abused me for years. The woman who thought me I couldn't truly trust anyone." He shrugs. "I just don't see the sense of moping around and rehashing things I can't change, you know. Because despite what anyone outside may think and all the rumors, I'm learning that sometimes it can be good to let a select few in. Because, I tried, and now I have you. At least, I want to have you."

His gaze meets mine. "Do you want to be my girlfriend?"

I smile. "Blaine Eric Dixon, are you asking me to go steady?" I tease, making Blaine return my smile.

"I guess I am," he confirms. "That is if you're willing to give it a try."

"I'd be willing to try anything with you," I say.

Our lips meet then, a sweet and tender kiss. Blaine's lips are insistent yet tender against mine, a soft press of warmth that sends shivers of anticipation down my spine. I respond with equal fervor, parting my lips slightly to welcome him. His tongue meets mine, dancing a slow, intoxicating tango that sends fireworks crackling behind my eyelids. The world around us fades away until there is nothing but the rhythm of our heartbeats matching the cadence of our kiss.

His taste, a unique blend of mint and the faintest hint of coffee from the cappuccino he'd had earlier, is intoxicating. I find myself drawn deeper, losing myself in the sweetness and warmth that is uniquely Blaine. His mouth explores mine with a gentle curiosity that speaks volumes about his care for me.

Blaine's hand drifts upwards from my stomach, over the curve of my waist and rests on the small of my back, anchoring me to him. The other hand is warm and firm at the nape of my neck, fingers tangled in my hair, holding me close.

My fingers clutch at the fabric of his shirt, pulling him even closer, wanting no distance between us. I run my other hand through his hair, relishing the kinky strands beneath my fingers. The sweet agony of wanting him, of wanting this to be something more, fills me with an overwhelming sensation of heat and longing.

My heart blossoms, the protective shell I'd built around it slowly starting to crack. In this moment, I fully surrender and it's both terrifying and exhilarating. Each caress, every whispered promise between shared breaths, becomes a promise of a future I can't help but want. I realize, with a jolt of clarity, that my emotions for Blaine are deepening beyond simple attraction. It's a dizzying realization, like stepping off the edge of a cliff and finding wings I didn't know I had.

A delicious ache builds inside me as Blaine's hands roam over my body, relearning the curves and planes of my figure. Blaine groans, pulling me onto his lap to deepen the kiss. The hard ridge of his arousal presses against me.

"Talia," Blaine breathes, his voice rough with need. He trails hot, open-mouthed kisses over my jaw and down my neck, pausing to nip at the fluttering pulse in my throat. "I want you so so bad."

"Then take me," I whisper, tangling my hands in his hair. "I'm yours, Blaine. Only yours."

CHAPTER 14

BLAINE

*I*t has been two whole weeks since Latalia agreed to give being in a relationship with me a try and it's been bliss. Of course, it helps that I have been booked and busy, but though I hate to admit it, it's also been because of the therapy sessions I'm now attending twice a week. Latalia has been working her magic both in my daily life and in the press as the stories have finally started to swing in my favor. This weekend is planned to be a big one for us as we're going public, and I know the press is going to eat this up.

Latalia leans over the kitchen island, scribbling notes onto the pages spread before her. Her hair falls forward, a puffy curtain shielding her face from view. I catch a whiff of her jasmine shampoo and fight the urge to bury my nose in her hair.

We've been at this for hours, going over possible interview questions they could ask later tonight as we meet with Vybe Magazine and how best to answer them. My responses sound stiff and rehearsed, even to my own ears, but Latalia insists authenticity and honesty are the best approaches.

"Relax," she says, glancing up at me. Her eyes are warm and knowing, seeing right through my anxiety. "Just be yourself. Let your personality shine through."

Easier said than done. I've spent years cultivating a public image that bears little resemblance to the real me. Latalia knows this, has witnessed firsthand the demons I battle daily. Yet she still believes I'm capable of change, of growth, in a way no one else does. *Not even me.*

I rake a hand through my hair and sigh. "I don't know if I can do this."

Latalia straightens, abandoning her notes to give me her full attention. Concern clouds her gaze. "You can. I know you can." She reaches across the counter to squeeze my hand. Her skin is soft and warm, her grip strong and sure. It steadies my frayed nerves. "You're talented, kind, hardworking. Any publication would be lucky to feature you. Just relax and be your charming self."

Her faith in me is humbling. I cling to her hand like a lifeline, drinking in her strength and confidence. With Latalia by my side, I feel capable of anything. Including baring my soul to the world.

"Okay," I say. "Let's go over the questions again."

Latalia's answering smile is radiant. My heart stutters at the sight. Together, we forge ahead. She reviews the list of sample questions the interviewer provided, quizzing me on possible answers. I stumble over a few that have to deal with my mom or my past, falling back on rote responses I've given in the past. Latalia calls me out on it each time.

"Be authentic," she chides gently. "Share your truth, not what you think people want to hear."

I scowl at the notes in front of me. "The truth isn't always pretty."

"It doesn't have to be." Latalia abandons the questions to cup my face in her hands. I freeze at the contact, caught in her hypnotizing gaze. "You are a complex, multi-faceted person. Let all sides of you shine through—your humor, passion, intelligence. Speak from the heart and people will see the real you, imperfections and all."

Her faith in me is humbling. And terrifying. To bare my soul to the world risks judgment and ridicule. But with Latalia, I feel safe. Seen and accepted for who I am. If I can bring even a fraction of that honesty and vulnerability to the interview, it'll be my most authentic one yet.

I cover her hands with mine, holding them in place. "What would I do without you?" The words slip out before I can stop them. Heat creeps into my cheeks.

Latalia's eyes soften. She brushes her thumb over my cheek, a feather-light caress that steals my breath. "Be good to me, and you won't have to find out."

My heart kicks into overdrive. Seeing Latalia in her element like this makes me think of how amazing a future together long term could be. Helping her achieve her dream of expanding her PR firm, and me finally doing something with that damn business degree of mine.

I know the therapist said to let things flow naturally with Latalia, and not let my mind stray to all that could be. But I'd be lying if I said I no longer got glimpses of hope that she could be my forever person I'd be told so many times I'd never have. I cling to her promise, the lifeline that tethers me to possibility.

I clear my throat and pick up where we left off. "You said improving professional relationships isn't about changing who I am. What did you mean by that?"

"That's the one question clients would ask me to clarify all the time. It's about finding common ground and showing mutual respect. Compromise when you can, without compromising your values." Latalia taps the paper between us. "For example, the interviewer wants to discuss your mom and dating life. Rather than refusing to answer or getting defensive, steer the conversation towards your passion for your work and future goals. Show interest in the interviewer and ask them questions too. Build rapport."

Her advice makes sense. I've pushed back on personal questions in the past to maintain boundaries, but that approach has likely come across as standoffish.

"I can do that," I say. "What else?"

"Make eye contact, smile, and listen actively. Repeat the interviewer's name occasionally, to personalize your responses." Latalia ticks off each point on her fingers. "Thank them for their time at the end of the interview. And if there are people on set for the photoshoot, introduce yourself and start a conversation to help yourself relax. Simple things, but they make a difference."

I shrug. "Those are all doable." The knot in my gut loosens.

I meet her gaze, hoping she sees my resolve. "I appreciate you pushing me. You're right, I can stay true to myself and also be respectful. I'll do my best to put your advice into practice. For you."

Latalia's eyes shine with pride and something more elusive I dare not name. Yet. She reaches across the table and squeezes my hand. "You've got this. Now, let's go over your goals for the interview one more time..."

We spend the afternoon working together, going over interview questions and responses, planning different outfits for the photoshoot, and prepping the house to be the perfect set.

By the time the first wave of the Vybe crew arrives, both Latalia and I are dressed and ready. We greet them at the door and Latalia takes a seat next to the director as they set up in the living room for the interview.

The interviewer, a petite woman with tanned skin and sharp features, perches on her chair with an eagerness that barely disguises her predatory instinct. She starts with the harmless questions: recent photoshoots, future projects, plans for personal growth. Her attitude is both professional and surprisingly cordial, creating an atmosphere that feels comfortable, even warm.

"Now, Blaine," she then turns the conversation towards trickier territory. "There's been plenty of speculation about your past and personal life, particularly about your relationship with your mother…"

I sit up straighter, a rehearsed smile on my face. But beneath the practiced veneer, there's something new – an authenticity that Latalia has helped me discover.

"My mother and I," I begin cautiously, "like any family, have had our ups and downs. She was and remains my biggest supporter. My past actions weren't always a reflection of the respect and love I have for her."

The interviewer leans in, intrigued by my response. I use the opportunity to steer the conversation away from my mom, bringing up my upcoming charity event. It's an obvious deflection, but one handled tactfully enough that the interviewer doesn't press the issue.

We segue into discussions about my bad-boy reputation, my image in the press, and the trouble I'd been in before. Each slanderous question is met with a diplomatic answer. I admit to my previous lack of discipline and express my commitment to personal growth. At one point, I even manage to lighten the mood with a joke about my former self, eliciting laughter from the interviewer.

"Sounds like you've changed quite a bit, Blaine," the interviewer comments, crossing her legs and leaning in closer. "Would this have anything to do with a special woman in your life?"

A knowing smile plays on my lips. "Actually, there is someone who's made a significant impact on my life."

"Would that be the renowned PR consultant, Latalia Brown?"

she pounces on my statement, her eyes alight with eagerness for the exclusive revelation.

"That would actually be spot on," I confirm, feeling a rush of excitement. "We are together and incredibly happy."

A flurry of excitement rushes through the room at my admission, and the interviewer quickly calls for a commercial break, promising our audience more exclusive details about my relationship with Latalia when we return.

As the cameras cut off, Latalia, who's been observing from the sidelines, gives me an approving smile. She joins us on set, ready to face the camera as my official partner. She gives my hand a gentle squeeze as she slides in next to me, leaning into my embrace.

The interviewer moves to have a spirited discussion with the director who glances in our direction before nodding in response to whatever the interviewer asked.

"Ignore them," Latalia whispers. "You're doing great."

I plant a light kiss on her cheek as the interviewer returns to her seat and takes a sip of her water before diving back in.

"So, Latalia, tell us about how you met Blaine, and how you've managed to tame our notorious bad-boy?"

Latalia laughs lightly, her calm demeanor in stark contrast to the tense atmosphere. "We actually met at an event about a few months ago, our chemistry was undeniable, and the rest was history. As for 'taming' Blaine, I think he's just been misunderstood. I've always seen the passionate, caring man he truly is."

The interviewer delves deeper, asking about Latalia's background in PR, how she maintains her composure, and what she brings to the relationship. Latalia answers each question with confidence and grace, casting our relationship in a new light for the viewers.

Then, to our surprise, the interviewer unveils a fun twist. "We have a game," she announces, producing two buzzers that were definitely not there before. "We're going to test how well you two really know each other. To level with you the buzzers are just for added fun. So, think fast, answer honestly, and may the best partner win!"

The game begins with rapid-fire questions, and we find ourselves laughing as we buzz in our answers.

"What's Latalia's favorite breakfast food?" the interviewer asks.

I hit the buzzer. "A full plate of bacon, eggs and Honey Blueberry pancakes."

Latalia laughs, nodding in agreement.

"And Blaine's go-to midnight snack?" The interviewer asks.

"Toast with almond butter and honey," Latalia answers without hesitation after buzzes.

The questions continue, revealing even the smallest details we've observed about each other.

"Blaine's most frequently worn color?" The interviewer asks, turning to Latalia.

"Black," Latalia declares, her smile radiant. She slams her hand on the buzzer and I laugh.

"You're supposed to hit the buzzer before you answer," I yell. "I get that point."

"I did," Latalia protests, knowing full well she didn't.

Our light rivalry is contagious as the whole crew laughs.

The interviewer turns to me. "Latalia's favorite song?"

"'Yellow' by Coldplay," I answer confidently.

"He didn't hit the buzzer," Latalia yells.

I slam my hand on the buzzer, laughing as I stake my protest.

By the time the game wraps up, we are both grinning widely, surprised and delighted by the depth of our knowledge about each other. The studio crew and interviewer clap enthusiastically, sharing in our joy.

"Wow," the interviewer exclaims, "It's clear to see you two are definitely 'couple goals'. I, for sure, hear wedding bells in your future. Remember viewers, you heard it here first."

I glance over to Latalia at the announcer's proclamation expecting to see terror at the mention of wedding bells but what greets me is a warmth that makes me forget about the cameras and the viewers. All that matters in that moment is the bond we share, now public and undeniable.

CHAPTER 15

The warm water cascades over my body as I drop to my knees, Blaine's thick, erect cock pulsing in front of my face.

"Fuck, baby, you're so fucking sexy." Blaine growls, fisting his hand in my wet hair.

My pussy clenches at the sound of his gravelly voice and the tug on my scalp. I gaze up at him through my lashes, watching as his pupils dilate with lust when I swipe my tongue over the swollen head of his cock.

The bitter, salty taste of his pre-cum bursts on my tongue and I moan before taking him fully into my mouth.

"Shit, just like that." Blaine hisses when I swallow him down to the hilt, his cock hitting the back of my throat.

I set a brutal pace, hollowing my cheeks as I suck and stroke him. My phone starts ringing on the counter, the loud, jarring sound interrupting us.

Blaine frowns and stills my head. "You should get that."

I pull off his cock with an audible pop, a string of saliva still connecting my lips to the tip.

"It can wait." I rasp, then dive right back in.

The phone continues to ring, ignored, as I lose myself in the feel and taste of Blaine's cock. His hands tighten almost painfully in my hair, hips bucking as he starts to truly fuck my mouth.

I moan wantonly around him, the sounds vibrating along his length. I can feel his thighs tensing, his balls drawing up tight against his body. He's close.

"Fuck, I'm gonna cum." Blaine grunts, giving one last hard thrust.

His hot release floods my mouth and I greedily swallow every last drop.

I stand up on shaky legs, wiping my mouth with the back of my hand.

Blaine pulls me into his arms under the spray of the shower, kissing me deeply. I taste myself on his tongue from earlier and I moan into his mouth.

My phone starts ringing again on the counter, the incessant sound breaking the moment.

Blaine pulls back with a frown. "You should really get that, babe. It could be important."

I sigh, knowing he's right. "It's probably just Jaden again. He's been blowing up my phone all day."

Blaine's eyes darken at the mention of my ex. "If he's bothering you, I'll put a stop to it."

"I can handle Jaden." I assure him, stepping out of the shower to grab a towel.

Wrapping the towel around myself, I check my phone to find several missed calls and over a dozen texts from Jaden.

JADEN:
Please talk to me.

· · ·

JADEN:

  I'm sorry, okay? I never meant to hurt you.

JADEN:

  Lala, baby, don't do this. We can work through this.

JADEN:

  Damn it, answer me!

I DELETE the messages without responding, dropping my phone back on the counter.

When I turn around, Blaine is there. He pulls me into his arms, not seeming to care that he's still dripping wet.

"You didn't deserve to be treated that way." he says softly, tucking my head under his chin.

"I know." I sigh, melting into his embrace.

"Do you want me to say something to him? Tell him to back off?" Blaine asks, his tone taking on an edge of steel.

"No, just leave it. I can handle Jaden." I repeat, tilting my head up to meet his gaze.

"If you're sure." Blaine concedes, though he doesn't sound happy about it.

"I'm sure." I assure him, standing on my toes to press a soft kiss to his lips.

He deepens the kiss, his hands sliding down to grip my ass through the towel. I moan into his mouth, getting aroused all over again.

Blaine breaks the kiss, resting his forehead against mine. "Round two?" He asks with a cocky grin.

"Definitely." I purr, dropping my towel to the floor.

Blaine scoops me up into his arms, carrying me into the bedroom. He lays me out on the bed, climbing over me to cage me in with his body.

"How did I get so fucking lucky." He growls, capturing my mouth in a searing kiss.

His cock is already hard again, rubbing against my inner thigh. I wrap my legs around his waist, grinding my pussy against his length.

Blaine tears his mouth from mine with a groan. "Shit, baby, you're gonna make me cum before I'm even inside you."

I smirk at him, rolling my hips to increase the friction.

He catches my hands, pinning them above my head. "Behave." He warns, though his eyes are dancing with laughter.

"Make me." I challenge.

Blaine's eyes darken, a predatory grin spreading across his face. He uses his grip on my hands to push me further up the bed, until my arms are fully stretched above my head.

Reaching down, he rubs the head of his cock through my slick folds, circling my clit. I whimper, trying to buck my hips, but he holds me in place.

"Oh, you naughty, naughty girl." He rasps. "You don't get to cum until I say so."

I groan in frustration, glaring up at him. He just smirks down at me, continuing to tease my pussy with his cock.

When I'm trembling and desperate, Blaine smiles, slipping on a condom and finally pushes inside me with one hard thrust. I cry out at the sensation, the stretch and burn of him filling me so completely.

He sets a brutal pace, pounding into me as I writhe beneath him. The restraint on my hands and the denial of my orgasm have me balancing on a knife's edge.

"Please." I beg, not caring how wanton I sound. "I'm so fucking close."

Blaine's rhythm stutters, his hips snapping against mine. "Not yet." He grunts.

I clench around him, reveling in the groan it pulls from his lips as I cum around his cock, trembling and screaming in pleasure. The final clench pushes him over the edge, and he finds his own release.

"Fuck," he grunts, as I smile.

"You play too much," I reprimand teasingly. "You're gonna be late for your shoot."

"Totally worth it," he quips.

He leans in to kiss me again and I slap him on the shoulder.

"Oh no you don't," I say laughing. "I've got to get some shots for social media before the shoot starts. We can't afford to be late. Not today."

"Fine," Blaine says with a devious grin. "But I'm calling in my rain check as soon as I get home tonight."

I laugh and give him a light kiss. "I could accommodate that."

It takes us a record forty minutes to shower again and get dressed. We get to the set with fifteen minutes to spare, which is perfect for me. I snap my shots and find a small desk in the back of the room to sit and work on admin stuff where Blaine goes off to get ready for the shoot. Watching from the sidelines, I can see he's a whole new man, his attitude on set is top tier. He makes a conscious effort to improve his attitude towards the crew and I smile, feeling proud of his growth.

Blaine walks onto the set of his photoshoot with a polite smile and greets the other models warmly. "Morning everyone. Hope you all had a good weekend."

A few of them look at him with surprise, clearly not used to his friendly demeanor. But they greet him in return, the tension in the room easing. Throughout the shoot, Blaine compliments his fellow models and engages them in casual conversation. He even offers to help one of the newer models with a difficult pose, explaining how to make it look more natural.

My heart swells with affection for him. I know how much courage it takes for him to open up to others and be vulnerable. The fact that he's pushing past his comfort zone to build better relationships with his co-workers shows me how much our talks have helped.

When the shoot wraps for the day, Blaine comes over to me with a shy smile. "How did I do?"

I wrap my arms around his waist, gazing up at him proudly. "You were amazing, babe. I'm really proud of you for putting in the effort."

Blaine's smile widens, his eyes shining. "What can I say? You've made me into a better person."

"You've always been a good person." I insist. "I'm just helping you see that."

Blaine kisses me one final time before squeezing my ass cheek then turning to head off to his dressing room.

My phone rings out as he turns to leave, and I tell him I'll be right there. I glance at the caller ID and see Jaden's name flash across the screen.

With an annoyed sigh, I answer. "What do you want, Jaden?"

"Lala, please just hear me out." Jaden pleads. "I'm so sorry for everything. Your assistant meant nothing to me, it was just a stupid mistake. I'll sign my position at the company over to you, I don't even care about that anymore. Just give me another chance to prove my love to you."

I scoff, shaking my head as if he can see me. "You must really think I'm real stupid. I will never trust you again after what you did, and there is no 'proving your love'. We're over, Jaden. Accept it and fucking move on."

"You can't deny that we had something special!" Jaden argues. "I made a mistake, yes, but we can work through it. Think of everything we built together. You know you still love me, Lala. I'm the only one who will ever truly love you. Not like that stupid model you're parading around with. As if a model could ever love you."

Jaden's words make me bristle with anger. But I pull in a steadying breath, refusing to allow him the satisfaction of affecting me or pulling me out of character ever again.

A bitter laugh escapes from my lips. "The only thing we built was a house of lies." I snap. "Whoever I decide to fuck, or love is my business. I will never go back to your manipulative bullshit. So, I suggest you go find yourself another bitch to get lost in. We're done here."

I end the call before Jaden can get another word in. With a relieved sigh, I look up to find Blaine coming back.

"Everything okay?" He asks in concern.

"Everything's perfect." I assure him, taking his hand in mine. And it's the truth. My past is behind me, and the future I want is right in front of me.

Blaine smiles, bringing my hand to his lips for a gentle kiss. "I'm glad to hear that. You deserve to be happy."

His words warm my heart. After everything I've been through, Blaine's care and belief in me is a soothing balm. The photoshoot wraps up shortly after, and Theo invites Blaine and I out for drinks to celebrate.

We step into the dimly lit bar across the street, following Theo as he leads us to a private booth in the corner. The bar is filled with a comfortable, friendly hum of chatter, laughter, and clinking glasses. A football game plays on the TV screens, but the patrons seem more interested in their companions and drinks.

"Best wings in town." Theo promises, sliding into one side of the booth with the other two models slipping in next to him.

Blaine and I share the other side, settling into the worn but comfortable leather. A waitress approaches, her eyes going wide when she recognizes the models. Theo orders a round of beers and two orders of wings, one spicy and one barbecue.

The beer is cold and refreshing, the first sip loosening the remaining tension from all the shit with Jaden. By the time the wings arrive, everyone is in high spirits, jokes and banter flowing easily between us.

Blaine surprises me by not only joining in on the fun but leading the charge on several occasions. The other models join in, their laughter filling the booth. We're all just people enjoying each other's company, the high-pressure world of fashion momentarily forgotten.

Ben, one of the other models, leans back in his seat with a grin. "I gotta admit, Blaine, I had you all wrong."

Blaine raises an eyebrow, swiping a napkin over his mouth. "Oh?"

"Yeah." Ben nods, tipping his beer bottle towards Blaine. "Always thought you were unapproachable, distant. But you're actually a pretty cool guy. Wish we could've broken the ice sooner."

The rest of the model murmur their agreement, and Blaine looks genuinely surprised.

"Well, I guess it's never too late to make new friends." He shrugs, offering them a small smile.

Everyone cheers to that, clinking their beer bottles together.

The night continues in a similar vein, all of us eating wings, drinking beer, and chatting up a storm. As the night grows later, Theo finishes his beer and slides out of the booth.

"I'm all 'socialed' out." he announces, stretching his arms over his head. "It's been a fun night, guys. But I need some beauty sleep."

A chorus of goodbyes and laughs follow his departure, and soon enough, the other models follow suit. Blaine and I are left alone in the booth, the remnants of our meal in front of us.

He leans over, pressing a soft kiss to my temple. "I had a good time tonight."

"So did I." I smile up at him, reaching out to squeeze his hand.

"You were amazing, Blaine. The way you opened up tonight...I'm proud of you."

He smiles. "It's all thanks to you." Blaine releases a shaky breath. "I've been thinking maybe it's time for you to meet my mom … while she's in her right state of mind." He hesitates. "If you want to. I've arranged for her to move over to the new care facility on Saturday. So, maybe we could set up something before that?"

He studies me. His mom was a big deal to him, despite all he'd been through. And if this is an important step for him, I'm willing to make it happen.

"Let's do it," I confirm, smiling up at him.

"Yeah?" he asks, happy surprise etched on his face.

I nod.

The barmaid approaches, asking if we want another round. But we decline, deciding to call it a night and head back home.

BLAINE

Saturday comes quickly. Latalia stands at the counter in my kitchen, stirring something savory in a pot. There was about ninety minutes left for our scheduled visit with my mom and already whatever she was whipping up to take with us smelled heavenly. The aroma of garlic, tomatoes, and spices wafts through the air, my mouth watering in anticipation.

I walk up behind her and slide my arms around her curvy waist, nuzzling the back of her neck. Her skin is soft and warm, flushed from the heat of the stove.

"Smells delicious," I murmur against her throat.

She leans back into me with a contented sigh. "Your favorite. Shrimp creole."

"You spoil me." I kiss the tender spot under her ear, eliciting a soft gasp.

"Only because you deserve to be spoiled." She turns in my arms and loops hers around my neck. Her lips curve in a teasing smile. "Especially today, and all the 'work' you've done."

I groan as desire pools low in my gut. We'd spent most of the afternoon in bed, our bodies entwined in a slow, sensual dance. The memory of her soft cries and the feel of her inner muscles clenching around me is enough to make me hard.

"Keep teasing me like that and we won't make it to dinner," I warn, sliding my hands down to cup her ass.

She laughs, the sound as rich and sweet as melted chocolate. "As tempting as that sounds, we need to eat. Plus, you've been really looking forward to us having this time with your mom. Are you still up for this? If you changed your mind, I'd understand. You come first in this scenario."

Her concern makes my chest tighten. I kiss her forehead, her nose, and the corner of her mouth. "You're the reason I want to be better. For you, I'd do anything. But tonight, is more for me. It's time to start the healing process. I'm just happy you'll be there with me."

She gazes up at me, her dark eyes shimmering. "You already are better, Blaine. You've come so far since we met. I'm so proud of you."

Her words threaten to undo me. I cling to her, overwhelmed by the feelings I'm developing for this incredible woman. She holds me close, her hands stroking my back. "I'm really falling hard for you," she whispers.

"I'm falling too," I tell her. "So damn much."

The time that it takes to get to the hospice goes by in a blur. The transition from Saturday morning to the hospice room is as swift as it is jarring. The mouth-watering aroma of Latalia's shrimp creole grapples with the harsh sterility of the room, battling to create an atmosphere that somehow feels both familiar and foreign at once. Every clink of the folding table as we set it up echoes through the silence, the past and the present coming together in this moment of truth. I can feel the tension threading through my muscles, a taught bowstring ready to snap.

Latalia, though, is a beacon. A flame in the muted colors of the hospice, her very presence a salve against the sharp edges of my fear. The moment she steps into the room, the air shifts, becoming something warmer, softer.

My mother lies in the bed, fragile and ghost-pale against the stark white sheets, her eyes widening as we enter. She surveys Latalia, a new element in her world, before her gaze falls on me. For the first time in what feels like forever, a genuine smile pulls at her lips.

The word "Mom" leaves my lips with a tremor. It's more than a simple greeting; it's a dam holding back years of pent-up pain, about to burst open with the introduction of Latalia into my past's bleak canvas. The lump in my throat is a tangible reminder of the gravity of this moment.

Beside me, Latalia stands like a lighthouse in the stormy sea of my past, her touch anchoring me to the present. She steps forward, a woman crafted of strength and resilience, her warmth washing over the room, daring to challenge the icy sterility that has long held dominion.

"Mrs. Dixon," Latalia greets, her voice a symphony of gentle power, wrapping the room in a soothing embrace, "it's a pleasure to meet you."

My mother, a woman who's lived in the shadows of her regrets, studies Latalia with a guarded gaze, a veneer of suspicion fogging her eyes. "Likewise," she responds, the word slipping from her lips with a barely concealed apprehension. Yet, I see a glimmer in her eyes, a spark of curiosity ignited by the enigma that is Latalia, a woman who's chosen to love the son she had once damaged.

The silence that blankets the room as we sit for dinner is thick, almost tangible. It hangs heavily over us, only to be displaced by the alluring scent of Latalia's shrimp creole. It wafts through the sterile room, a rebellion against the chill, an unspoken promise of something warmer, something better.

"I hope you enjoy the meal, Mrs. Dixon," Latalia's voice breaks the silence, her words a soft hymn that seems to reverberate against the cold walls. "Blaine told me you were partial to Creole food."

A murmur of appreciation escapes my mother's lips, her tense demeanor losing a bit of its rigid edge, replaced by a cautious curiosity. "Thank you," she whispers, almost to herself.

As we delve into the meal, I find myself an onlooker in the quiet transformation unfolding in the room. My mother's defenses, built over years of guilt and regret, start to crumble under the onslaught of Latalia's gentle persistence. Each spoken word, each shared look, pushes her further into the realm of vulnerability, chipping away at the icy exterior that's kept her at arm's length for so long.

Emboldened by the softening atmosphere, I seize the moment to broach a topic that's been a specter hovering over us.

"So, I've been going to therapy," I say with Latalia's reassuring grip serving as my anchor.

"Oh," my mother says, glancing in my direction before returning to her food.

"Yeah," I continue. "I've been working through some of the stuff we've been through in the past."

My mother turns to me with a look of terror. She opens her mouth to speak, but no words follow.

"Mostly on forgiveness, and the prerequisites of healing," I continue. "What I've learned is that in order for me to fully heal and truly move on with my life I need to forgive you for all the shit that happened."

The silence that ensues is monumental. It engulfs us, a storm brewing in the air, laden with the weight of my revelations. The resignation and defiance swimming in my mother's eyes feel like a silent acknowledgment, but I need her verbal assurance that she understands where I am and that there will be a long road ahead.

"Look, I'm not saying I'm there yet, because I know I'm not. But I'm willing to try if you are."

"I understand, Blainey," she murmurs, her voice a frail whisper that gets carried across the room.

"I'm going to be holding you accountable this time," I clarify. "This is your last chance to prove to me to value your family more than the shit you keep putting in your body. I don't like the person you become while your own that stuff, and there are no more free passes for the things you do when you're drugged up." I meet her dead in her eyes. "Mom, I'm serious about this. I've found a long-term facility just outside of Manhattan that has a rehab facility and medical staff that can help you get back to yourself. Now it's not cheap, but I am willing to cover the costs for as long as you're remaining committed to the program."

My mother nods.

"But the moment I get a whiff that you're back to your old antics, that's gonna be it. I won't keep funding your relapses." I sigh. "And both Blair and I agree that if you don't commit to getting yourself better, you can't continue to be apart of our lives."

"Okay," she says after a moment of silence. "I can't lose my boys again. I be better. I promise."

I nod, taking her words for what it is for now as a small smile kisses the corners of her lips.

What follows feels like a dream. Laughter, warm and heartfelt, rings through the room. Stories, punctuated by moments of shared understanding, fill the air. This version of my mother, this softer, humble avatar, feels simultaneously alien and familiar. This semblance of normalcy, this tentative step towards domesticity, strikes a stark contrast to the turmoil that's been our shared past.

As we re-enter the house, the last strains of "At Last" by Etta James paint the air with a sense of poignant finality. We had forgotten to switch off the music before we left but now it serves as the perfect backdrop to end the day. I pull Latalia closer with the melody fading into silence as we slide onto the couch.

"That was perfect," Latalia murmurs.

"It was." I breathe in the scent of her hair, stroking my hand down her back. "But the night's still young."

She looks up at me, eyes gleaming. "Is that right?"

I dip my head and brush my lips over hers. "If you're interested, I have a few more things in mind to make this an evening you'll never forget."

"By all means," she purrs, "continue. I'm listening."

Before she can react, I kneel in front of her.

"Blaine, what are you—oh!" She gasps as I undo the button of her jeans and slowly unzip them. I look up to find her watching me, lips parted.

"Still listening?" I ask, sliding her jeans down.

She swallows hard. "Actively."

"Good." I dip my head to press a kiss to her inner thigh.

CHAPTER 17

LATALIA

In the two weeks since meeting with Blaine's mom, time has been moving like a whirlwind. After getting his mom settled in her new live-in facility, Blaine had gone away for a week to do a photoshoot out in L.A., and though he'd offered for me to go with him, I had jumped at the time to get a small reprieve with Trina and the girls plus some 'me time' which was heavenly.

It had felt good to have been able to make the choice to stay on my own instead of just running behind Blaine, like I once would have in my past relationship. For a moment I'd been worried that the time apart would've created a rift between us. But, in the week that he's been back we've been able to fit back together like a custom-made glove.

I don't wanna jinx this but dare I say it, Life is good.

The sun beats down on my bare shoulders as I lounge on the pool deck, flipping through the latest issue of Vogue that my man is both on the cover off, and on the center spread. My eyes glaze over the glossy two-page photo of Blaine clad in a dangerously sexy tuxedo without an undershirt when real life Blaine emerges from the house, phone in hand and a devilish grin on his lips.

"Blair's on the line. He's invited us to some fancy art show and party tonight. Apparently, they'll be hors d'oeuvres and champagne."

I look up to study his face for a reaction. I know enough about Blaine to know that if he's coming to me to pitch the idea while Blair is still on the phone it's because he doesn't really wanna go and needs me to be the excuse.

Blair's voice registers through the receiver once more and Blaine rolls his eyes.

"Blair would like me to inform you that there will also be tons of press and opportunities to get shots of me painted in a good light."

I laugh. "Tell him we'll be there."

"What are the magic words?" He holds the phone just out of reach, a tease of a smile playing at the corner of his mouth.

"Please?" I arch a brow, unable to keep from smiling back. "Before I change my mind?"

He shakes his head and I roll my eyes, laughter bubbling up from my gut. "And we'll still have our 'naughty nightly routine' after."

Blaine chuckles, leaning down to drop a soft kiss on my lips. "Bingo." He returns the phone to his ear. "She says you're in luck. We'll see you tonight."

He ends the call, slipping the phone into his back pocket before settling into the lounge chair beside mine. I close my eyes, soaking in the warmth of the sun and Blaine's presence.

"You're going to melt out here." Blaine's fingers ghost over the back of my hand, a whisper of a touch. "Come inside?"

I crack one eye open to find him watching me, a hunger in his gaze that has nothing to do with the sun. Desire kindles within me at the promise in his eyes.

I laugh, swatting his arm playfully. "Nice try. We already promised Blair we'd go."

Blaine groans, dragging a hand through his hair. "Can't we just stay here? I'm not really in the mood for one of his parties."

"It might be fun!" I stand, holding out a hand to help him up. "Besides, you know how much this means to him. We haven't been out together in weeks."

Blaine's lips twist into a pout, but he takes my hand and pulls himself to his feet. "Fine. But you owe me."

"I'll make it worth your while." I grin, grabbing his shirt to pull him down for a searing kiss.

By the time we break apart, Blaine's frown has melted away. He shakes his head, a rueful smile tugging at his lips. "You do drive a hard bargain, Talia."

I pat his chest, already turning towards the house. "Now, let's get ready. We've got an art party to attend!"

Blaine follows behind me, muttering under his breath about manipulative women and their wiles. I hide my smile, knowing that despite his protests, he enjoys these nights out together as much as I do.

After a quick shower, I make my way to the closet, sorting through dresses and heels. I settle on a stunning emerald-green dress that Kamilla had gifted me for my last birthday, the silky fabric clinging to my curves.

I turn to grab a necklace from my vanity, catching Blaine's reflection in the mirror. He's leaning against the doorway, arms crossed over his chest as his gaze rakes appreciatively over my body.

Heat floods my cheeks when our eyes meet in the mirror. Even after all this time, the weight of his desire still has the power to unravel me. I clear my throat, fumbling with the clasp of my necklace. "See something you like?"

Blaine pushes off the doorway, his fingers grazing my neck as he takes the necklace from my hands. "Very, very much so." His voice is a low rumble against my ear, sending a shiver down my spine.

Warm lips trail over my shoulder, unhurried and thorough. I close my eyes, tilting my head to give him better access. The necklace falls from my fingers, forgotten.

"We're going to be late," I breathe, even as I arch into his touch.

"So?" Blaine nips at the sensitive skin below my ear before smoothing it with his tongue. "I'd rather stay here and peel this dress off you."

I laugh, breathless as I turn in his arms. He's already shirtless, and I splay my hands over the hard muscle of his chest, tracing the lines of his scars. "Tempting, but Blair would never forgive us."

Blaine sighs, ducking his head to steal a proper kiss. I melt into him, my hands winding around his neck to pull him closer.

We break apart, both breathless. Blaine rests his forehead against mine, his eyes closed. "I swear you're going to be the death of me."

"But what a way to go," I tease, smoothing a hand over his cheek.

Blaine's eyes snap open, a wicked grin tugging at his lips. "Indeed."

He releases me with obvious reluctance, grabbing a button down from the closet and shrugging it on. I turn back to the mirror, securing a pair of statement earrings.

By the time we're ready, Blair has called twice to check on our progress. Blaine laces his fingers through mine, bringing my hand to his lips.

"Ready for an interesting night?"

I smile up at him, giving his hand a squeeze. "With you? Always."

We arrive at the gallery to find it already packed with people. Loud music pounds through the speakers, the bass vibrating in my chest. Waiter's weave through the crowd carrying trays of champagne flutes and hors d'oeuvres.

Blair spots us immediately, rushing over to greet us. "You made it!" He envelops me in a hug,

"Don't you look stunning?"

I laugh, unable to contain my smile. "Thank you. You look rather dashing yourself."

He straightens, smoothing a hand over his tailored suit with a wink. "Why thank you, darling. Come, there are some people I'd like you both to meet."

Blaine tenses beside me, his fingers tightening around mine. I glance up at him, brows furrowing a tad. He offers me a strained smile, the tension in his jaw belying the casual gesture.

Ah. Of course. Blair's "people" are most likely more models and socialites - the type of crowd Blaine typically avoids for fear of being objectified or taken advantage of.

I squeeze his hand, hoping to ease some of his discomfort. To my relief, he seems to relax, some of the tension seeping from his shoulders.

Blair leads us over to a pair of men engrossed in conversation near a large abstract painting. "Cole, Seth, I'd like you to meet Latalia."

The men turn, appraising me openly in a way that sets my teeth on edge. Beside me, Blaine tenses again, his hand clenching around mine.

Cole, the shorter of the two with stylishly messy brown hair and sharp, cunning eyes, offers me a lazy smirk. "Well, hello there." His gaze trails over me appreciatively before flickering to Blaine. "Aren't you going to introduce us to your date, Blaine?"

Blaine's jaw clenches, his irritation apparent. "This is my girl-friend, Latalia."

The emphasis on the word "girlfriend" is unmistakable, a clear warning for the men before us. Cole's smirk falters briefly before returning, though it doesn't quite reach his eyes.

"Lovely to meet you," Seth interjects, perhaps hoping to diffuse the tension. He offers me a polite smile and a handshake which I return.

"Likewise," I say, meeting Cole's gaze evenly.

Cole's eyes gleam with poorly veiled contempt as he drawls, "So, you're the one who finally tamed our wild stallion. Color me impressed."

His words cut, meant to demean, and diminish our relationship. I grit my teeth against the urge to snap back, to put this arrogant jerk in his place. Beside me, Blaine goes rigid, rage simmering beneath the surface.

I squeeze his hand in warning, a silent plea for him to remain calm. We can't afford a scene, not here, not now. Taking a steadying breath, I offer Cole a tight smile. "Taming Blaine was hardly necessary. We share a connection borne of mutual trust and respect."

Cole scoffs, clearly unconvinced, but before he can issue a biting retort, a familiar voice cuts through the din.

"Well, isn't this cozy."

My heart leaps into my throat at the sound of that smooth, confident baritone. Against my will, my gaze flickers to the entrance, finding the source of that voice without fail.

Jaden.

He stands in the doorway, clad in an expensive designer suit, scanning the room with a predatory gaze. Beside him, dressed in a revealing red dress, is my ex-assistant, Shelby. She clings to his arm, gazing up at him as if he was God's gift to man.

I grind my teeth, bile rising in my throat, as Jaden turns his head, pinning me with a triumphant smirk.

Beside me, Blaine stiffens, rage simmering in his eyes as he takes in the scene before us.

The air around us grows tense, a palpable silence falling over our group as Jaden approaches.

"Well, well, if it isn't Latalia," Jaden purrs, his eyes raking over me. "Aren't you a vision in that little dress? Pity you'll always be trash beneath the finery."

My cheeks burn at the insult, at the accusatory stares and poorly concealed smirks of those around us. I bite my tongue to refrain from snapping a retort, knowing it will only spur him on.

Beside me, Blaine bristles, rage simmering in his eyes. His fingers tighten around my waist in a gesture meant to comfort, but there's tension in his touch, a volatile energy thrumming through him.

Jaden, of course, remains oblivious to the warning signs, too drunk on his own hubris to realize he's pushing Blaine too far.

"Tell me, Blaine," he continues, in a mocking facsimile of concern, "how does it feel to spread the legs of my sloppy seconds?"

The crude remark elicits gasps and titters from onlookers, their discomfort and derision rankling. Again, heat floods my cheeks as I fight to rein in my anger.

All the reasons I left Jaden coming flooding back to my mind. All the years spent diminishing myself to suit his whims. Of feeling powerless. Voiceless.

No fucking more.

I lift my chin, meeting Jaden's sneer with a defiant gaze. "He wouldn't know," I reply coolly. "Blaine satisfies me in ways you never could."

Rage flashes in Jaden's eyes, his composure fracturing for the briefest of moments.

Beside me, Blaine relaxes marginally, a surge of pride rolling off him in waves. He presses a swift kiss to my temple, the gesture possessive. Protective.

Jaden sputters indignantly, clearly struggling for a response.

Before he can craft a suitable retort, Blaine levels him with a withering glare. "I suggest you leave. Now. While you still can."

"Yeah, cool it Jaden," Blair adds. "This is not the place."

Jaden ignores Blair, his eyes locked on Blaine's. For a tense moment, it seems Jaden will call Blaine's bluff, too arrogant to back down from a challenge. Shelby tugs insistently at his arm, her expression pinched with fear and concern, but Jaden pushes her off.

"You think because you're having fun sucking on this asshole's cock, you can one up me bitch? What the fu —"

A loud crack of knuckles on bone echoes through the room as Blaine's right fist connects to Jaden's face before he could finish his retort.

My heart leaps into my throat. I should stop this. I need to stop this before someone gets seriously hurt. But my feet remain firmly planted, refusing to move from their spot. I can only watch with wide, helpless eyes as the violence unfolds.

Jaden clips Blaine on the jaw and he stumbles, off balance. Seizing the opportunity, Jaden tackles him to the ground where they grapple and snarl at one another like wild animals.

As I finally muster the courage to step forward, Jaden shoves me away. The action incites Blaine further, and before I know it, he's landed another blow on Jaden, knocking him out cold.

Blaine stands over Jaden's unconscious form, chest heaving from exertion and rage. Slowly, the anger bleeds from his expression, replaced by dawning horror at what he's done.

He glances up at me, eyes wide and imploring. "Talia, I didn't mean to..."

I rush forward and wrap my arms around him. "We should get outta here."

The stunned silence that had engulfed the room is shattered by the flash of camera bulbs, a flurry of activity as reporters scramble to capture the dramatic scene.

My stomach drops as the implications set in. This will be plastered across every tabloid and gossip site by morning, Blaine's reputation in tatters. His career could be over because of me.

I turn to Blaine, clutching at his arms with trembling fingers. "Now. Blaine. Let's go."

He nods mutely, gaze still fixed on Jaden's prone form.

I give him a little shake, forcing his attention to the present. "Blaine. Look at me."

He does, eyes meeting mine. There's a storm of emotions raging within his eyes.

"We'll figure this out," I assure him. "But we have to leave. Please, just trust me."

He nods again, and we make our way to the exit, my mind buzzing with thoughts of damage control as I fish for my phone to warn Trixton.

CHAPTER 18

LATALIA

I roll out of bed, my head still buzzing from last night's shit show. I reach for my tablet, planning to check the time, but what catches my attention instead is a barrage of notifications from news sites and social media. I blink, bewildered as my own face, captured mid-punch, glares back at me from multiple tabloid headlines.

Dread fills me as I assess the aftermath. As expected, I'm fucked.

'*Second Public Assault: **Blaine Aldridge Unleashed Again!**'* one headline screams.

Another, '***Violence Unchecked: Serial Fist-Flyer Blaine Aldridge Strikes Again!***'

. . .

MY HEART LURCHES as I realize how the media is painting me. Just another violent celebrity, a loose cannon. My past mistakes served up fresh to the world.

'BLAINE STRIKES AGAIN'.

MY HANDS TIGHTEN around the edge of my tablet as I scroll through the rest of the headlines. More phrases like *"model gone mad"* and *"roid rage?"* flash across the screen, accusations and speculation from people who have no clue what really happened.

I rub the ache building at the base of my skull, remnants of the blows I traded with that waste of space. The scene replays in my mind, his hands on Latalia's waist as he whispered in her ear, her obvious discomfort. I lost it, the anger bubbling to the surface in an uncontrollable swell.

Latalia.

Guilt twists in my gut at the thought of how I must have scared her, the violence I'm capable of when provoked. I can only imagine what she must think of me now, my barely contained rage and the beast that lurks just beneath the surface.

With a curse, I launch the tablet across the room. It crashes into the wall, the screen fracturing on impact. I ignore the stinging in my knuckles from the force of the throw, instead focusing on slowing my erratic breathing.

In. Out.

I need to make this right, to assure Latalia she has nothing to fear from me. To beg her forgiveness for the scene I caused and the way I must've frightened her. I have to convince her that she's the one thing keeping the beast at bay, her presence the only thing that soothes the savage inside.

My heart clenches at the thought of losing her, of having to face a world without her in it. She grounds me, gives me a reason to push the darkness aside. Without her, the beast wins.

Pushing out of bed I rush to find Latalia. I find her sitting at the kitchen table, her gaze fixated on her phone as she scrolls through the same tabloids. Worry lines are etched on her face, tension marring her usual composure. She looks up at me, and something inside me fractures at the sight.

I've done this to her. I put that look on her face and the slump on her shoulders.

Before I can speak, she looks up, meeting my gaze. "We need to talk."

My stomach drops at her words. I move to sit across from her, searching her face for any clue as to what's coming next. She takes a deep breath, steeling herself.

"Talia, I'm so sorry," I say, the words tumbling from my lips. "I never meant to frighten you like that. I lost control and took things too far, and I understand if you want nothing to do with me after this. But I'm getting help. I'm going to do better, be better for you."

"No Blaine, this is all my fault. I'm so sorry," Her voice barely more than a whisper. "I didn't know Jaden would go this far. He was still messaging me shit even this morning. I promise I will make it right."

Her eyes meet mine. It takes me a second to process.

"Jaden messaged you this morning?" I ask, a tight knot forming in my stomach. "You're joking right? Why the hell does he still have access to you right now? Why isn't he blocked?"

The words come out more forceful than I meant, hurt bleeding into my tone. She steps back, taken aback by the sudden outburst.

"Blaine, I've shut him down, every single time," she says, her voice steady despite the evident distress in her eyes. "I am all in on us, on you."

Her words hang in the air between us, their gravity pulling me towards her.

"Wait," I say, stopping short. "You said every time, as in more than once. How long has this back and forth between you guys been going on?"

Latalia takes a deep breath, her eyes not leaving mine.

"Truth," she said. "Jaden has been hounding me for months, calling and texting. I've shut him down every single time, but he just keeps coming back. I admit I could have blocked him. Or even deleted his number at some point."

"So, why haven't you?" Again, my tone comes out harsher than I'd like.

Her answer isn't immediate, and her hesitation slashes like a knife to the gut.

"Oh, my fucking God. Tell me you don't still have feelings for that moron."

"No," she confirms, without hesitation, easing my nerves.

"Then what is it then?" I ask with a sigh. "Why can't you just block him."

She shrugs and blows out a heavy breath. "I guess I was just too scared to block his number, because I was afraid of what he might do if he didn't get what he wanted. I honestly never meant for any of this to happen."

I don't know what I was expecting her to say, but fear wasn't it.

A tear runs down her cheek and I pull her closer to brush it away with my thumb.

"Please don't cry," I say, in a soothing tone. "I'm sorry, I didn't mean to make you upset."

She leans into me.

"I don't know all that happened between you and Jaden in the past but know that I'll never allow anyone to hurt you ever again," I assure her. "Especially that jackass. Okay?"

Latalia nods, meeting my eyes. "I'll block him."

I sigh. "Thank you."

My phone pings, and I pull it from my pocket to check.

"Great," I say with a sigh.

"What's wrong Latalia asks, angling her head to see my screen.

"The media is crucifying me. They now apparently have an inflammatory interview from Jaden." He sighs. "This could seriously damage my career."

"I'll take care of it," Latalia assures me. "I already have a plan in place with Trixton. This will blow over, I promise."

"Thank you," I say. "How can I help?"

A faint smile crosses her lips. "I think it's time you met my found family I told you about. The Sisterhood"

CHAPTER 19

BLAINE

The Sisterhood. The two words that have haunted me for the past seventy-two hours. These three people were the people who Latalia trusted the most in the world. And though meeting them turned out to be business related, it warmed me to think that Latalia was integrating me into her world as much as she was in mine. The plan is for Latalia to get some shots of me with her friends and family to show that I was unbothered by the rumors floating around. But I'd be lying if I didn't admit I was starting to have doubts that she was ready to let me in, and that thought plays on my nerves.

It's only human to wonder, had this whole debacle with Jaden not set off a press shit storm, would I even be meeting her family as she considers them? I've broken down all my defenses for her, but thanks to this whole scenario the illusive clouds of bliss have started clearing and I'm not sure I'm liking the realties I'm recognizing from the clear skies.

I follow Latalia into her old apartment, model smile in place.

Their home is filled with laughter and warmth. The smell of good food fills the air, and the sight of familiar faces immediately puts Latalia at ease.

My own nerves melt away with each step through the threshold. The tangy aroma of jerk chicken and rice and peas teases my senses, my mouth watering in anticipation. Dancehall music plays in the background, the heavy bassline pulsing through the floorboards and up my legs.

Latalia glances over her shoulder, flashing me a smile. "Relax. My girls are going to love you."

Her words do little to soothe my anxiety, my fingers flexing at my sides. I'm out of my element here, far from the sterile minimalism of my own home. But Latalia's hand finds mine, her fingers interlacing with my own, and just like that, a wave of calm washes over me.

"There's my baby sister!" Latalia pulls me forward as a curvy woman with a halo of curls turns around. They collide in a hug, Latalia nearly lifting the other woman off her feet. "Blaine, this is my sister, Trina."

Trina's eyes light up as she takes me in, her gaze lingering a beat too long to be polite. Heat rises to my cheeks, the intensity of her stare setting me on edge. But then she smiles, wide and bright, and pulls me into an embrace.

"It's so great to officially meet you," Trina says. "Tals hasn't shut up about you since she left."

I shoot Latalia a look, catching the hint of color staining her cheeks. She ducks her head, busying herself with the strap of her purse. The corners of my lips curve in a genuine smile. So, she does talk about me to them at least.

"All good things I hope," I say, hoping to get more details.

Trina giggles. "More devilish."

I raise an eyebrow before glancing over to Latalia who somehow manages to turn the melanin in her cheeks brown red.

Trina links her arm through mine, leading me further into the room. "C'mon, there are more people for you to meet."

Latalia snaps a picture on her phone before leaning in so we can hear her over the music. "Remember both your allegiances lie with me. She turns to Trina. "So, no embarrassing family stories from you." Then turns to me. "And no home secrets from you."

I shrug before turning to Trina with a cheeky smirk. "They are embarrassing stories?"

Trina laughs. "Whole heap."

Latalia's eyes widen as Trina pulls me away with a huge smile. I glance over my shoulder at her and wiggle my eyebrows and throw her hands up in surrender.

I let Trina guide me along, the tension in my shoulders fading with each introduction. By the time we make it to the kitchen, I'm laughing along with them, the heady blend of music, laughter and delicious smells making it impossible not to relax.

Maybe this won't be so bad after all.

Trina abandons me to help her sister in the kitchen, leaving me with Natasha and Kamilla. But their easygoing nature puts me at ease, drawing me into their conversation as if we've known each other for years.

"So how is it like living with Tals?" Natasha asks, refilling my glass.

I rub the back of my neck, heat crawling up my face. "Pretty chill, actually."

"Ooh, look at that blush!" Kamilla teases, nudging me with her elbow. "I'm sure it's 'super chill'". Sarcasm laces her tone. "You can't fool us mister. Spill."

"There's not much to tell." I clear my throat, avoiding their curious gazes. "Talia is amazing. I was hardly home before she moved in as, before her help, I had hardly been able to book repeat New York gigs. And I wasn't overly thrilled about her moving into my space at first either if I'm honest. But ..." I paused to glance over to the kitchen in the open concept and smile. "Something just clicked. And she grew on me."

"Just clicked, huh?" Natasha waggles her eyebrows at me, a sly grin curving her lips. "Is that what the kids are calling it these days?"

My face flames, the innuendo in her words hitting me like a ton of bricks. But before I can sputter out a response, raucous laughter fills the space between us. I stare at them, stunned, before realization dawns - they're joking. Teasing me to get a reaction.

Shaking my head, I take a swig of my drink, the burn of alcohol doing little to temper the heat in my cheeks. But beneath the embarrassment lingers a warmth in my chest, a giddy sort of happiness at their playful acceptance.

Latalia joins us then, slipping her arm around my waist in a casual display of affection that makes my heart skip a beat. Her touch is grounding, chasing away the last dregs of tension still clinging to my shoulders.

I glance down at her, at the smile she gives me, radiant and carefree as Trina calls us over to the dining table to dive into the meal.

Dinner is delicious. These women can cook.

"This is delicious Trina," I say, helping myself to a second serving of rice and peas. "And this gravy...spectacular. Did they cook a lot of Caribbean food while you were growing up?"

"Not really here in the states," Latasha clarifies.

"But our granny, back in Montego Bay," Trina added. "She could cook you into next summer."

Latalia's gaze meets mine. This is a new side to her for me. As she doesn't really talk about herself. The earlier thought of her not letting me in creeps back up in my mind but I push it back down.

"I didn't know you guys lived in Jamaica," I say, tilting my head hoping to appear less hurt at the lack of information I know about them.

Latalia and Trina burst out laughing.

"We didn't," Latalia clarifies. "Our mother was Jamaican, but we were born here in the states and only visited Jamaica once as teenagers for the summer break while our mother figured out her next move."

"Oh," I say, a bit relieved.

As if sensing my unease Latalia continues. "I hardly mention it because I feel like it would be an injustice for me to walk around claiming to be Caribbean, like this one does all the time," she pauses to teasing gesture to Trina. "When I've really only been there once and most of what we know are from books or the internet."

"And the summer with our granny," Trina corrects.

"Gotcha." I say. "That's understandable."

"They got the food bit locked down though," Kamilla added.

"And the dancing." Natasha added.

"Dancing, huh?" I ask, glancing in Latalia's direction.

Laughing, Latalia snaps a picture of us all laughing before excusing herself, retreating to the bathroom, and leaving her phone on the table.

My gaze follows her as she walks away, admiring the sway of her hips beneath the fitted dress she wears. When I glance back at the table, it's to find her friends watching me, amusement lighting their eyes.

Heat crawls up the back of my neck at being caught staring, but I shrug it off. "What? She's gorgeous."

Laughter meets my confession, loud and filled with joy. I duck my head. But there's no malice in their banter, no judgment in the way they tease. Just acceptance, open and honest in a way I'm not quite used to.

Latalia's phone rings out, the shrill sound cutting through the ambient noise of music and chatter. At first, I think nothing of it, telling myself whoever it is will call back. But then it rings a second time and I glance down to see the name flashing across the screen.

Jaden.

My heart seizes, anger and hurt rearing their ugly heads. Before I can stop myself, I reach for the phone, tempted to answer and give him a piece of my mind. But just as my fingers curl around the device, I come back to myself.

This isn't my place. Latalia left her phone behind, yes, but taking it upon myself to answer would only cause more trouble. No matter my feelings towards her ex, this is a line I can't cross.

Swallowing back the bitter taste in my mouth, I leave the phone where it lies. The sounds of laughter and music continue around me, but my focus remains on the phone and the name still flashing across its screen.

The phone finally stops ringing, the silence that follows almost as loud as its incessant sound. I glance around the table, noting the way conversation has continued without pause, no one else seeming to have noticed the call or my reaction to it.

Latalia returns, her smile fading as she picks up on the shift in my mood. She checks her phone, her face falling as she recognizes the caller.

Her eyes meet mine across the table, wide and pleading, an unspoken apology in their depths. I look away, jaw clenched, and take a long swig of my beer instead of responding.

The bitterness on my tongue does little to quell the anger burning in my gut, flames fueled by jealousy and a bone-deep possessiveness I've never felt before. Latalia is mine, and the thought of Jaden thinking he still has any claim on her paired with the knowledge that despite her empty promises he still hasn't been blocked makes my blood boil.

Without a word to me, she tells her friends that a work emergency has occurred, and we need to leave early. I follow her lead, keeping my anger in check until we're out of earshot.

Latalia steers me toward the front door, hand warm on my arm, each step ratcheting my temper up another notch. It's not until we're outside, the door clicking shut behind us, that I turn on her with a snarl.

"You didn't block him." My voice is deceptively calm despite the rage churning inside, a veneer of control over the violence threatening to break free. "After everything, you still didn't fucking block him."

She winces, dropping her hand from my arm. "I'm sorry, I forgot. I'd left his number up so I could try to build the courage up to request my client list. I tried calling his dad, but he directed me back to Jaden. But I couldn't call at that point. Then so much started happening with us, and things have been going so well, it just slipped my mind." Latalia bites her lip, gaze darting away. "I never thought he'd actually call again."

"But he did." I step into her space, crowding her against the wall of the house, hands braced on either side of her head. She's trapped, and still, I resist the urge to do something I'll regret. "He's always going to call Latalia. He's always going to find a way back into your life until you cut him out for good."

My heart hammers against my ribs, fury, possessiveness, and my feelings for her a tangled mess inside my chest. She's mine, but until Jaden is gone for good, I'll never really have her. Not the way I want. Or the way we both need.

She swallows hard, eyes flicking up to meet mine. "You're right." Her admission is soft, laced with guilt. "I should have blocked him a long time ago. I'm so sorry, Blaine."

I nod, jaw clenched. Sorry doesn't cut it, not this time.

"I don't know what else to say." Latalia lifts her hands, hesitating before settling them on my chest. Even that small point of contact is enough to soothe my frayed nerves. "I messed up. I know how much stress and anxiety this causes you, and I should've put a stop to it."

Sighing, I close my eyes. The rage in my chest morphing into defeat. "You've been half in this whole time. Had the fight with Jaden not forced you too, I probably still wouldn't have met the people that mean the most to you. Let's face it, Talia. I'm not a priority in your life. But for once I need to put myself as a priority in mine."

Her hand stiffens on my chest. "Please, Blaine. Don't do this."

I blow out a breath and meet her eyes. "I can't do this anymore. You're great at your job and for so long you fought for this to remain that way. I should've listened. You can continue heading up my PR team for as long as you want the job. But this thing, whatever it is … or isn't between us, has to stop." I sigh. "Tomorrow, I'll figure out a set contract duration for your live-in assignment so you can get back to your family as soon as possible."

Her face goes pale, but I turn to go to the car before she can answer or I can give in and pull her back into my arms to comfort her, telling myself this is for the best.

The drive back home passes in tense silence. I keep my hands clenched on the steering wheel, jaw tight, as the memory of Jaden's name flashing across Latalia's phone plays on a loop in my mind.

By the time we pull into the driveway, anger has once more begun to simmer in my gut. I kill the engine and push open my car door, the creak of metal loud in the quiet night.

Latalia calls after me as I stalk up the path to our front door, but I don't turn back. Can't turn back. If I do, I know I'll say or do something I regret.

Keys jammed into the lock, I shoulder open the door and step into the house. The familiar warmth and lived-in comfort usually bring me peace, but tonight they do little to temper my foul mood.

Latalia's gaze sears into the back of my back, a weight that makes my skin prickle. When she steps up behind me, hand curling over my bicep, I jerk away. The hurt in her eyes makes me falter.

"Blaine, please talk to me." Her voice is soft, pleading. "I'm sorry. I know I fucked up, but we can work through this."

The fight seeps out of me, anger fading in the face of her distress. I've never been able to stay mad at her for long, but that doesn't mean I've forgotten. Not this time.

"I really am sorry." Latalia lifts her hands, hesitating before settling them on my chest. Even that small point of contact is enough to soothe my frayed nerves.

Sighing, I close my eyes. I want to stay angry, to rage and fume and make a point, but the fight bleeds out of me at her touch. She's not perfect, but neither am I. We've both made mistakes, and if I want this relationship to work, I have to learn to move past them.

"Just block him." My hands slide down to grip her waist, fingers digging in with bruising force. "Promise me you'll block him, and we can move on from this."

"I promise." Her answer comes without hesitation. "First thing tomorrow, his number is gone for good. No more contact, no more chances. I'm done."

Her words come like a punch to the gut.

"Are you fucking kidding me?" I ask, stepping away from her. "Tomorrow?"

Without another word, I storm off to my bedroom, slamming the door behind me. My chest heaves as I pace the confines of my room, anger and betrayal warring inside me. How could she do this? After everything we've been through, all the promises we made to each other, she still can't let go of him.

The image of his name flashing across the screen is seared into my mind. Jaden. Even now, the thought of him makes my blood boil. He's poison, a cancer that's intent on destroying everything good in my life, and Latalia can't see it. Or maybe she just doesn't want to.

I slam a fist into the wall, relishing the burst of pain that shoots through my knuckles. Anything to distract from the ache in my chest.

Latalia knocks on the door, her voice soft as she calls my name. I ignore her. I'm not ready to face her, not when I can still feel the ghost of his presence clinging to her.

"Please talk to me." The door creaks open, and she slips inside. I keep my back to her, jaw clenched. "I'm done with Jaden, and I want to make this right."

"Just leave me alone." The words come out harsh, biting, but I make no move to soften them.

She doesn't respond. I listen as her footfalls pound away further and further from the door, but I'm done fighting, I'm done competing. She needs to make a choice.

CHAPTER 20

LATALIA

J sink into the plush leather chair across from Dr. Reid and smooth my hands over my dress. The familiar anxiety bubbles in my stomach rise to the surface. I hadn't been in here for an in-person session since moving in with Blaine, and I'm still deciphering how I feel discussing him here knowing he's probably also been talking about me in his sessions.

It also doesn't help that I've missed about a month of sessions, but I've grown used to Dr. Reid's kind eyes and soothing voice. So hopefully that will make talking about my relationship issues with Blaine easier.

"How are things with Blaine?" Dr. Reid asks, as if reading my mind. She peers at me over the rim of her glasses.

I blow out a breath and shrug. "We're trying. It's been a rough couple of weeks."

"You mentioned in your last session that you two were just starting to get closer and struggling with communication. Have there been any improvements on that front?"

"Some." I twist my hands together, unsure of how much to reveal. Dr. Reid is easy to talk to, but this is deeply personal. Intimate. "We had been making more of an effort to really listen to each other. To be open and honest in a constructive way."

"That's excellent progress." Dr. Reid nods, scribbling something on her notepad. "Building trust and improving communication are the foundations of a healthy relationship."

"I know." I give her a weak smile. "Easier said than done."

"Of course. These things take work." She regards me steadily. "But it seems you and Blaine are putting in the effort. And that desire to make your relationship a priority will serve you well." She pauses. "I notice, however, you said 'had'. Are you no longer working on your communication?"

Of course, she heard the 'had', nothing passes her.

"Thing have been ... strained in that department between us lately," I admit.

Communication had literally been virtually non-existent, but I couldn't bring myself to admit that. The half-truth made me feel like shit as there was no way to really be helped if I wasn't honest.

Dr. Reid studies me before scribbling something in her notepad. "Crafting personal relationships is hard, often regardless of how pure our intentions are. Getting one that works to last long-term takes work and disagreements are inevitable. They're part of life. What matters is how we learn from them and what we do with that new knowledge we've gained. So, if a successful relation is something you really want then go for it with all your might."

Her words lift some of the weight from my shoulders and I sit up straighter. She's right. Blaine and I both want this, and we're willing to do whatever it takes to make things right between us.

With that resolve strengthening inside me, I dive into the details of the past two weeks with Blaine, starting with the fight between Blaine and Jaden and the events that unfolded in the weeks that followed, sharing both the good moments and the bad. Dr. Reid listens as she always does. Patient. Non-judgmental.

By the time our session ends, I feel lighter. Hopeful. Like maybe, just maybe, Blaine and I will be able to move past this rough patch after all.

That night, I try to wait up for Blaine, but I fall asleep before he gets home, and he leaves for work the following morning before I wake up. When I go downstairs, there's a note on the kitchen counter in rushed handwriting:

LATALIA,

EARLY MEETING THIS MORNING.

-BLAINE.

I STARE at the impersonal note, a rock settling in the pit of my stomach. Four words. That's all he had for me after I bared my soul in therapy yesterday. Sure, he wouldn't know that. But he would if he'd stop avoiding me.

I scrunch the note in my fist. So much for progress. I sigh. Why didn't I just delete Jaden's number when I realized there was no way in hell, I was getting back that client list? It was a stupid oversight. I just wish Blaine would at least give me a chance to apologize.

When Blaine slips through the front door late that night, I pretend to be asleep on the couch. Pretend I don't feel the chasm widening between us as he walks by the stench of alcohol lingering behind him with each step. I know starting a conversation with him at this point will go nowhere.

In the morning, he's gone again before dawn. No note this time. No goodbye kiss. Just the imprint of him in the house, already fading.

I sit at the kitchen table with tears burning my eyes, wondering how we ended up here. Wondering if there's any way left to bridge the distance keeping us apart, or if this is what love looks like when it falls apart.

CHAPTER 21

My heart hammers against my ribcage as I step through the threshold of Blair's apartment, a cacophony of panic threatening to overwhelm me. Latalia's face flashes in my mind, her warm brown eyes brimming with hurt and confusion, full lips trembling as she struggled to hold back tears. I shake my head roughly, trying to dislodge the memory, but it only sinks its claws deeper into my consciousness.

I slump onto the worn leather couch with a groan, pressing the heels of my palms against my eyes. How did everything spiral out of control so quickly? One moment we were curled up together, lost in a haze of bliss, and the next...

"You look like shit."

I drop my hands to find Blair leaning against the arm of the couch, arms crossed over his chest. Annoyance and concern bouncing off his expression, the latter emotion evident in the crease between his brows.

"Thanks," I mutter, "I feel great."

Blair snorts, settling into the space beside me. "Cut the sarcasm. What happened?"

I open my mouth, then close it again. How do I even begin to explain the disaster that has been the last two weeks? That I let my jealousy and pride get the better of me, and ended up pushing Latalia away?

Blair nudges my shoulder, brows raised in question. I release a sharp breath, raking a hand through my hair.

"Latalia and I had a fight," I admit finally. My chest constricts at the words, as if voicing the truth aloud makes it more real. More painful.

"About what?" Blair presses. I know he won't let this go until I give him the full story.

"Her ex that she's still obviously caught up on," I say through gritted teeth. The memory of Latalia's phone buzzing on the table, Jaden's name flashing across the screen, ignites a flare of anger in my gut all over again. "She promised me after the art show debacle that she's block the fucker. But she didn't and led me to believe that she had. When I saw his fucking name flashing on her caller ID." I shake my head. "I just...lost it."

"You overreacted," Blair states bluntly. I bristle at his accusation, opening my mouth to protest, but he continues before I get the chance. "When are you going to accept that Latalia's past is her own? That you can't control who contacts her or when?"

His words strike a chord in me, resonating with an unpleasant truth I don't want to face. I shake my head again, harder this time, and reach for the bourbon on the table. Maybe if I drink enough, I can drown out the echo of Blair's voice in my head.

The bourbon burns a trail of fire down my throat, but it does little to quiet my racing thoughts. I can feel Blair's gaze on me, his frustration mounting with each swig I take from the bottle.

When I finally meet his eyes again, his lips are pressed into a thin line. "You're going to drink yourself to death at this rate," he says bluntly. "And for what? Because you can't get over your own insecurities long enough to see what's right in front of you?"

His words cut deep, slicing into wounds that have never truly healed. I surge to my feet, the room tilting dangerously around me as the alcohol hits my system.

"You don't know anything about this," I snarl.

"I know you're a damn fool if you let Latalia go over something so trivial!" Blair shouts, rising to meet me. We stand chest to chest, anger and frustration simmering between us, tension as thick as the bourbon clouding my senses.

In my drunken haze, the walls of the apartment seem to close in around me. The echo of Latalia's laughter rings in my ears, a ghostly reminder of all I stand to lose.

"I can't do this again," I whisper, shoulders slumping in defeat. "I can't give her my heart only to have it shattered into pieces."

"Latalia isn't like our mother," Blair says firmly. "When are you going to see that she's different?" He grasps my shoulders, giving me a rough shake. "When are you going to see that she loves you?"

I pull away from Blair's grip, turning to stare out the window at the city stretched out below. My reflection gazes back at me, haunted eyes peering out from beneath the jagged scar marring my cheek.

"She still talks about him, you know," I say softly. "Every time we're together, Jaden's name slips past her lips like a reminder of what we can never have. How am I supposed to build a future with a woman so caught up in her past?"

A bitter laugh fall from Blairs lips. "That's rich coming from you seeing you're still caught up in your own shit. You still see every woman through the lens of what mom did to us." Blair's voice is gentle yet firm. "Latalia is nothing like her. She chose you, scars and all, and she wants a future with the man you are now, not the boy you once were."

His words strike deep, piercing the walls around my heart. I know he speaks the truth, have always known deep down, yet voicing those fears has been too painful to bear. Latalia claimed my heart from the moment I saw her, larger than life and radiating warmth, a stark contrast to the cold loneliness I'd grown accustomed to.

"I was a fool to push her away," I whisper, eyes burning with tears I refuse to shed. "She's the best thing that's ever happened to me, and I destroyed us over my own fucking insecurities."

Blair rests a hand on my shoulder. "Give her some time. She loves you - she'll come around."

I shake my head, throat tight. "You didn't see her eyes. The hurt in them..." I trail off with a shuddering breath. "I really messed this up."

"So, make it right." Blair squeezes my shoulder. "Apologize. Tell her you were an idiot, and that you never want to lose her again. Fight for her."

I pull Blair into a fierce hug. "Thank you."

He hugs me back just as hard. "Anytime."

"I'm going to make this right," I vow, meeting Blair's gaze steadily.

A slow grin spreads across his face. "About damn time."

"After I sleep off this alcohol," I clarify.

We both laugh as I collapse back onto the couch, a smile on my lips as I let the darkness of sleep wash over me.

CHAPTER 22

LATALIA

I sit in Blaine's living room, nerves fraying with each minute that ticks by. This has gone on for far too long. He didn't even come home last night, and thoughts of what could've happened to him wrecked my mind all night. Calling him has yielded no results either. No call. No text. Just silence.

Radio silence.

When the front door opens, I jump to my feet as anger and hurt curdle in my stomach. Blaine stops short in the doorway, surprise flickering over his face before his expression softens.

"We need to talk," I say, my voice trembling. "We can't go on like this."

He hesitates, jaw clenched, and for a moment I think he won't accept my apology. Then his shoulders slump in defeat. He looks exhausted, weary lines etched into the handsome planes of his face. But his eyes are alert and wary. Waiting.

"Blaine, I—" My voice cracks, and I swallow hard. "I'm so sorry."

Silence. He watches me, unmoving, as the seconds tick by. Waiting. Judging.

I take a deep breath and steel my nerves. It's time to lay all my cards on the table. To beg for forgiveness and pray for another chance.

Pray he gives me the opportunity to make things right.

"I was wrong," I blurt out. "So wrong. I hesitated to block Jaden's number. If I had done it right when you asked, I wouldn't have forgotten. That was on me. I promise you I have zero feelings for Jaden. Deep down I knew Jaden had no intentions of releasing my old client list, yet I still let him manipulate me to believe there was a chance. I should have been able to put our relationship ahead of his games. I see that now."

Blaine's expression doesn't change. He walks over and sits. But he doesn't interrupt me. Doesn't tell me to stop.

I take that as encouragement and surge onward. "You're the one I want, Blaine. You're the only one I've wanted since the moment we met. I was confused and hurting, and I made a mistake. A huge mistake that I regret every single day."

My eyes burn, tears welling up and spilling over before I can stop them. I reach up to swipe at my cheeks but Blaine brushes them away with his thumb before I can. I hate how emotional I'm getting but I push on. I stare at Blaine through the veil of tears, heart in my throat, waiting for his response. Hoping I haven't ruined everything between us for good. He tenses but doesn't pull away as I take his hand in both of mine, clutching it close to my heart.

"I choose you, Blaine. I'll always choose you. I'm done with the past, done with lies and secrets. I want a future with you."

His eyes lock on mine.

I take a deep, steadying breath and meet Blaine's gaze. His expression softens, giving me the courage to push on.

"When I first came to you, I told myself you were just a

distraction. A way to get over Jaden and move on with my life." I give a humorless laugh, shaking my head. "You were never just a rebound, Blaine." I laugh to myself. "Not that I didn't try. And heaven knows I had never in million years anticipated I'd end up working for you, let alone living with you. But you became a light that pierced through the darkness in my soul. You saw beyond the walls I'd built around myself, saw the woman I could be. And you loved her, insecurities and all, in a way no one else ever has."

I reach out, taking his hands in mine. They're warm, strong and calloused in all the right places. Familiar. Reassuring. "I tried to fight it, to cling to the lies I'd told myself. But I just can't anymore. I'm in love with you, Blaine. I love your passion and intensity. I love how I can be fully myself around you, flaws and all, knowing you'll still accept me as I am."

Tears blur my vision as I search his face. Hoping, praying I'll find the same depth of feeling reflected in his eyes. "Loving you terrifies me," I admit softly. "But not being with you, that would destroy me."

Blaine closes the distance between us in a heartbeat, his hands coming up to cup my face. I gasp at the intensity in his eyes, the raw emotion that threatens to undo me.

"I love you, Talia," he says, his voice rough. "So damn much. I'm sorry if I ever made you feel otherwise. I spent so long going back and forth ridiculing myself for loving you when I thought you didn't feel the same way. But I have loved you from the moment I saw you in that lousy club. I love you with every fiber of my being."

His lips are on mine in a hungry kiss. The world fades away. The kiss is insatiable, a perfect mix of desperation and longing. His hands, strong and warm, cradle my face, drawing me closer into the vortex of his magnetic pull.

I'm lost in the rhythm of the kiss, every other thought pushed away by the taste of him on my lips. His breath mingles with my own need and desires as though all the oxygen in the room has been replaced this fervent, all-consuming kiss.

Blaine pulls back, breathless, resting his forehead against mine. His eyes remain closed as he takes a deep, steadying breath. When they open again, the shadows haunting them have faded, leaving his gaze clear and bright.

"The past few weeks have been hell," he admits. "When we weren't together, it felt like the sun didn't exist. The light just...went out of my world." He shakes his head. "I told myself I didn't need you. That I was better off on my own. But the truth is, I was drowning without you."

His hands slide down to grip my shoulders, squeezing tight. "I retreated into myself. Started drinking to numb the pain, the loneliness. Before I knew it, I was staying with Blair more often than not, waking up bitch faced drunk on his couch or floor." He swallows hard. "Anything to forget you. To forget how much it hurt."

His hand slides up to cradle the back of my head, his touch infinitely gentle. "You're the best thing that's ever happened to me. The thought of losing you, of you moving on with someone else..." He shudders, eyes squeezing shut. "It damn near destroyed me. I won't make that mistake again. I'm here, Talia, and I'm yours. For as long as you'll have me."

I surge forward, crushing my lips to his. There is desperation in the kiss, all my fear and pain bleeding out as I pour my heart into it. Blaine meets me measure for measure, the hand at my neck keeping me close as if afraid I'll disappear.

We break apart, breathless and clinging to one another. I lay my head over his heart, listening to its steady beat. Soothing and constant.

"I'm yours too, Blaine," I whisper. "Always have been. Always will be."

Blaine lifts me into his arms, our lips finding each other again as he carries me upstairs to the bedroom. Each step elicits a soft moan from me, the friction of our bodies and the heat of his mouth setting my blood aflame.

By the time we reach the bed, we're both panting. Breathless with need and desire. Blaine sets me down to remove his shirt, the sight of his sculpted torso and washboard abs sending a fresh wave of arousal coursing through me.

My hands roam across the firm planes of his chest, tracing the faint silvery lines of old scars. Marks of battles won and lost; private pains etched into his skin.

Blaine stills, eyes searching my face. Waiting.

I press a soft kiss above his heart, over the deepest scar. A silent promise to cherish every part of him.

With a groan, Blaine claims my mouth again. His hands slide under my dress, fingers dancing across my thighs. I whimper as he finds my center, already wet and aching for his touch.

"So perfect," he rasps, stroking my slick folds. "So beautiful, Talia. All of you."

I moan, arching into his fingers as they slip inside. The fullness, the delicious stretch leaves me trembling, craving more.

Blaine adds another finger, his thumb circling my clit in a slow, maddening rhythm. I rock my hips, chasing the building pleasure, every nerve in my body attuned to his skillful touch.

"Please," I gasp, clutching at his shoulders. "I started the pill. I want to feel your cock inside me."

Blaine pauses. "Are you sure?"

"Yes."

The word is his undoing as he lifts me again, guiding me onto his lap as he sits on the edge of the bed. Our mouths fuse together as I position him at my entrance, slowly sinking down onto his thick, hard length.

The feeling of him filling me, stretching me, hits me like a lightning bolt.

We stay there for a long moment, joined in the most intimate way, savoring the connection. Blaine cups my face, gazing into my eyes with a tenderness that makes my heart ache.

"I love you," he whispers.

Tears well in my eyes as I cling to him. "I love you too. More than anything."

Blaine kisses me softly, gently rolling his hips. I moan against his mouth, rocking with him, setting a slow, unhurried pace.

Each thrust sends ripples of pleasure through my body. The delicious friction, the slick slide of him inside me, builds and builds until I'm trembling on the edge of release.

"Cum for me, baby," Blaine rasps, holding me up so he can thrust deep into me and back out. "I want to feel your juices around me."

His words push me over, and I shatter in his arms. Waves of ecstasy crash over me as I clench around Blaine's cock, crying out his name.

With a groan, Blaine follows, spilling inside me in hot, wet spurts. We cling to each other as the tremors fade, breaths slowing, hearts beating as one.

After a long moment, Blaine lifts me gently off his lap and onto the bed. He curls around me, pulling me close, one hand resting over my hip.

"Thank you for giving me another chance," he whispers against my hair. "I love you so much, and I'm never letting you go again."

I lace my fingers with his, pressing deeper into his embrace. "You're have my whole heart, Blaine."

In the silence of the night, wrapped in Blaine's arms, I know that this is where I'm meant to be. Home.

EPILOGUE

BLAINE

The morning sun filters through the blinds as my phone starts ringing, jolting me awake. Trixton's name flashes across the screen.

I grab the phone, my heart already racing. "Trixton, what's going on?"

"Blaine! I have incredible news." Trixton's usually composed voice is laced with excitement. "The Calvin Sparrow movie we've been hounding on for months? It's yours. They also want you to be the face of their new men's fragrance."

My eyes widen as I sit up straighter in bed. "What? Are you serious?"

"Dead serious. You killed it in the final audition. This is huge, Blaine. This is the kind of campaign that will skyrocket your career to the next level."

I run a hand over my head, stunned. Months of prep and practice have paid off. I visualize the campaign in my mind, my face plastered on billboards in Times Square. The thought sends a thrill through me.

"I don't know what to say," I tell Trixton. "Thank you. For pushing me, for believing in me, for getting me this far."

"You can thank Latalia." He laughs. "You earned this, Blaine. No one deserves it more. Now go celebrate with Latalia!" Trixton says warmly. "You two have had a lot to celebrate recently. I'll be in touch with the details."

We end the call and I fall back onto the bed, staring at the ceiling. Latalia stirs beside me and opens one eye.

"Who was that?" she mumbles sleepily.

I roll over and pull her into my arms. "You're looking at the new star of the upcoming Calvin Sparrow movie and the face of their men's fragrance."

Latalia's eyes fly open as she pushes up on her elbows. "What? Blaine, that's amazing!" Her full lips curve into a radiant smile and she throws her arms around me. "I'm so proud of you, baby."

I hold Latalia close, relishing her warmth and the feel of her soft skin against mine. "We did it," I whisper into her hair. "All the hard work, all the struggles, it's finally paying off. And I couldn't have done it without you by my side."

Latalia pulls back to gaze at me, her eyes shining. She brushes her lips over mine in a sweet, tender kiss. "Here's to new beginnings."

I return Latalia's kiss, savoring the taste of her lips. "New beginnings," I echo.

My phone buzzes again with an incoming text. I glance at the screen and grin. "The studio wants to meet with you about handling PR for the movie. Looks like your hard work is paying off too, babe."

Latalia's eyes widen. "What?"

My smile grows wide. "They want you too. Trixton just messaged me asking if I think you'd be interested."

"Oh my god, tell him yes." She says, her tone laced with enthusiasm.

I tap out a quick reply confirming her interest before setting the phone aside. "This is turning out to be the best day ever, and it's only just getting started."

Latalia laughs, the sound like music to my ears. "I'll say! So much for a quiet morning in bed." She slides her hands over my chest, her touch igniting my skin. "Since we're celebrating, how about we make the most of this perfect lazy day?"

Heat pools in my gut at the sultry tone of Latalia's voice and the hungry gleam in her eyes. I crush my mouth to hers, kissing her with a passion that steals my breath away. Our bodies press together, warm skin against warm skin, and a familiar ache stirs between my thighs.

Latalia moans into the kiss, her hands roaming over my body to grip my hips. I deepen the kiss, my tongue dancing with hers, as I settle more firmly between her thighs.

A throaty groan rumbles in Latalia's chest. She hitches one leg around my waist, rocking her hips to grind against my stiffening length. The friction sends sparks of pleasure rippling through me, and I break away from her lips to gasp.

"Too many clothes," Latalia murmurs, her fingers working at the drawstring of my sweatpants. She shoves the fabric down until my erection springs free, hot and throbbing against her thigh.

I bury my face in the curve of Latalia's neck, nibbling at her silky skin as she takes me in hand. Pleasure swamps my senses at her firm, knowing stroke. "God, Latalia." My voice comes out ragged. "You're going to be the death of me."

"But what a way to go," she teases, her hand picking up speed.

I clench my jaw, heat and tension coiling in my balls as Latalia works me closer to the edge. This woman will be the absolute death of me, but I wouldn't have it any other way.

I break away from Latalia's embrace, ignoring her noise of

protest. "As tempting as this is," I say, tugging my sweatpants back into place. "We have things to celebrate."

Latalia pouts up at me, looking thoroughly debauched with her mussed hair and swollen lips. "We were celebrating."

"We haven't even had dinner yet." I drop a quick kiss to her forehead and move off the couch, holding out a hand. "Come on, I'll make your favorite."

With an exaggerated sigh, Latalia allows me to pull her upright. "You're no fun." But her lips quirk into a smile and she follows me into the kitchen.

While Latalia sets the table, I gather ingredients for my special Chicken Parm. My hands move on autopilot, dredging chicken pieces in flour and spices. In the background, Latalia's phone chimes repeatedly with incoming calls and messages.

We carry our plates into the dining room, the table laden with more food than we can possibly eat. But that's the point - we have so much to celebrate, why hold back?

I fill Latalia's glass with wine, my nerves jangling like a nest of snakes as I consider the ring burning a hole in my pocket. There's no reason for her to refuse. I mean we've discussed marriage before, and she's made it clear she wants a future with me.

Still, doubts plague me. What if it's too soon? What if she's not ready? I shake off the worries, reminding myself that we've been through too much together to hesitate now. Latalia is it for me, and if she needs more time before making it official, I'll wait. I have forever to convince her, if necessary.

"You're quiet," Latalia observes, spearing a mushroom cap. She chews thoughtfully, then adds, "Something's bothering you. Tell me."

Trust Latalia to see right through me. I grasp her hand, threading our fingers together. "Just thinking about how far we've come," I say honestly. "And how much further we have to go."

Latalia squeezes my hand. "Together," she says simply.

The snakes in my pocket settle at her affirmation. I lift my glass, waiting until Latalia does the same before speaking.

"To the future and walking each step of the journey hand in hand."

"To the future," Latalia echoes, "and to never letting go."

We drink, and when I set down my glass there's a new lightness to my movements, all doubts banished. Tonight, I will ask Latalia to be my wife. And by the love so apparent in her eyes, I already know her answer.

As I clear the plates, a soft melody fills the room. I had purposely left out the vinyl with Latalia's favorite R&B songs knowing that she wouldn't be able to resist putting it on. Latalia turns to me with a twinkle in her eyes as 'Always' by Pebbles fills the room, an invitation for a dance.

My heart stutters, then kicks into overdrive. This is the perfect moment. I deposit the plates in the sink before returning to her with an outstretched hand, unable to keep the grin from my face. Latalia's fingers curl around mine and I pull her close, one hand finding the familiar curve of her hip, the other clasping her hand against my chest.

We sway gently, Latalia's head resting on my shoulder. Her hair tickles my neck, its fruity scent wrapping around us. I drop a kiss to her temple, squeezing her tighter against me.

"Remember the first time we danced?" I ask softly. "Seems so long ago now."

Latalia hums. "You were terrified of stepping on my feet." A huff of laughter escapes me from the memory. I had been hopeless, stumbling over my own feet in my anxiety.

"You were very patient with me," I say. "You're always patient."

"You were worth the effort," Latalia replies, tilting her head up to meet my gaze. Her eyes are soft. "You still are."

My breath catches at the raw emotion in her voice, in her eyes. This is it. The perfect moment I've been waiting for. I stop moving, taking Latalia's hands in mine.

"I have something for you," I whisper, nerves and excitement filling me. I slide one hand into my pocket, fingers closing around the velvet box.

Latalia's eyes widen, her lips parting in a gasp. "Blaine, what —"

I sink to one knee, gazing up at the woman who holds my heart, my future, my everything.

"Latalia Elizabeth Brown," I say, flipping open the box to reveal the diamond nestled inside. "You have been the first thought on my mind every morning since walking into my life, and the last thought putting a smile on my face before I go to bed at night. My life would be meaningless without you. Will you make me the happiest man alive and marry me?"

She stares at the ring, then at me, tears gathering in her eyes. For a long moment she says nothing, and my heart lodges in my throat. What if this is too soon? What if—

"Yes," Latalia breathes. A radiant smile lights up her face as a tear slips down her cheek. "Yes, Blaine, I'll marry you."

Joy and relief surge through me and I rise to my feet, pulling her into my arms. Our lips meet in a searing kiss as she wraps herself around me, pouring what feels like a year's worth of love, passion and promise into one kiss.

When we part, I cradle her face in my hands, brushing away her tears with my thumbs. "I love you so much," I whisper, resting my forehead against hers. "You're the best thing that's ever happened to me. I want to spend the rest of my life proving that to you."

"You already have," Latalia says. She kisses me again, swift and sweet. "A thousand times over. I love you with all my heart, Blaine Dixon. Always have, always will."

I slide the ring onto her finger, a perfect fit. Just like us. Two halves of one whole, now and forever.

A LETTER TO THE READER

<u>Dear Amazing Human</u>,

Thank you so much for dedicating time out of your life to reading my book! I hope you found it entertaining and were able to have the good time that I had intended it to be.

If you enjoyed what you read, and have a few extra minutes, PLEASE drop a review on Goodreads and any book retailer of your choice. If you hated it … that sucks. I'd still love to know how I could make your experience better next time. So, please feel free to share your honest thoughts. I'm extremely grateful for you, and I hope you'll join me on the journey of my next release.

By the way, if you'd like to continue along with Latalia and Blaine to see what they got up to after the story, consider Joining My Newsletter so you can be notified of my upcoming release dates and special offers.

Hugs,

UP NEXT IN THE SERIES - BREAKING HER RULES: A BROTHER'S BEST FRIEND, ROOMMATES, FRIENDS WITH BENEFITS, SPORTS ROMANCE

Breaking Her Rules

Surviving a friends-with-benefits setup isn't rocket science if you stick to three rules:
  • Avoid people you work with - you don't want to mix business with pleasure.
  • Never choose a neighbor - you need peace at home.
  And the golden rule:
  • NEVER EVER FALL IN LOVE!

Sounds easy, right? My name is Kamilla Morallez, your quintessential sassy, Afro-Latina, and I don't just bend these rules, I incinerate them. Why, you ask?

Meet Jackson Taylor, the smart-mouthed, irresistibly charming quarterback and my brother's best friend, who is now my roommate whom I hate. As if that wasn't challenging enough, fate threw another curveball: he's now my physiotherapy patient. So, two rules down, and I've barely even started.

Sure, we began as rivals and moved on to a frenemies-with-benefits arrangement, and we know our boundaries. Or so I thought. The closer we get, and the more intense our passion becomes, the more my carefully drawn lines begin to blur. Suddenly, our 'simple' agreement transforms into an emotional labyrinth.

Great. Now, with two rules already shattered, I've got my work cut out for me because the last thing I need is to break rule number three.

***Breaking Her Rules** is a heart-pounding, enemies-to-lovers, brother's best friend, roommates, friends-with-benefits, forced proximity, athlete/physiotherapist contemporary romance with a guaranteed happily ever after. Each book in the Rules of Love series can stand alone and be read in any order. Please note: This book contains mature themes and adult language, with no closed doors in sight. Reader discretion is advised. ***

AFTERWORD

I want to thank God for blessing me with a fantastic support system and the strength to push forward in spite of it all.

I'm super grateful to my loving husband for all his support, feedback, and encouragement along my journey of losing myself in this story as it consumed me, and rediscovering who I wanted to be. It is impossible to produce a novel without the passion needed not only to write but also to market it. I will be eternally grateful for the pushing force you have been beside me on each leg along the way. I love you, baby!

To the amazing Teralyn Mitchell, I swear you have been a blessing, and I have no idea what I would do without you. Thank you for giving me the push I needed to get things back on track. Without you, these stories would just be sitting on my hard drive, begging to be released. You've always got a friend in me.

Ms. Lyra Parish (Courtney), thank you for being as selfless as you are and consistently sharing your knowledge, time, and magical writing sprints. I've almost written a million words with you, and I see many more in our future.

And finally, to all my remaining family members, friends, and readers from across the globe who continue to support me day in and day out, thank you for embracing the magic that evolves out of the craziness in my mind. I am beyond thrilled that you have decided to jump on this winding journey right along with me. Now hang on, as it's about to be a bumpy ride.

ABOUT THE AUTHOR

Deidre - Ann Anderson is a USA Today Bestselling author of everything romance with black women and the men who love them.

She is a Jamaican-born Canadian author who firmly believes that with hard work and dedication, anyone can make a living from what they enjoy.

Deidre – Ann has been a storyteller for most of her life and cannot wait to share all the rigorous love stories of the characters living in her head.

THANK YOU FOR YOUR SUPPORT!

To find out more about books, news, and more, sign up to *Dee's Writing Corner*!
* * * **Follow me on the socials** * * *

BookBub: https://www.bookbub.com/authors/deidre-ann-anderson
Facebook Reader Group:
https://www.facebook.com/groups/deidreannanderson-sreaderfam/
TikTok: https://www.tiktok.com/@deidrewritesromance
Author Newsletter: https://view.flodesk.com/pages/64a492bb349daf2cf867bb19
My Author Website: https://www.deidreannanderson.com
Instagram: https://www.instagram.com/deidrewritesromance